Claudia Piñeiro lives in Buenos Aires. For many years she was a journalist, playwright and television scriptwriter and in 1992 she won the prestigious Pléyade journalism award. She has more recently turned to fiction and is the author of the novel *Thursday Night Widows*, awarded the Clarin Prize for Fiction, and *All Yours*, both previously published by Bitter Lemon Press.

A CRACK
IN THE WALL

Claudia Piñeiro

Translated from the Spanish
by Miranda France

BITTER LEMON PRESS
LONDON

BITTER LEMON PRESS

First published in the United Kingdom in 2013 by
Bitter Lemon Press, 37 Arundel Gardens, London W11 2LW

www.bitterlemonpress.com

First published in Spanish as *Las grietas de Jara*
by Alfaguara, Buenos Aires, 2009

Bitter Lemon Press gratefully acknowledges the
financial assistance of Arts Council England

A CIP record for this book is available from the British Library
ISBN 978–1–908524–089

Typeset by Tetragon, London
Printed and bound by Cox & Wyman Ltd., Reading, Berkshire

LOTTERY FUNDED

Supported using public funding by
**ARTS COUNCIL
ENGLAND**

"Listen. Suppose this wasn't a crack in you – suppose it was a crack in the Grand Canyon."
   "The crack's in me," I said heroically.

The Crack-Up
F. Scott Fitzgerald

1

Pablo Simó is at his desk drawing the outline of a building that will never exist. He has been making the same sketch for years, like a man condemned to have the same dream every night: one about an eleven-storey tower facing north. There's a series of identical drawings in a file; he doesn't know exactly how many, he lost count a long time ago – more than a hundred, less than a thousand. They aren't numbered, but each one is dated and signed: Pablo Simó, Architect. If he wanted to know which day he drew the first one, he would need to find it and look at the date, but he never does that; the most recent bears today's date: 15 March 2007. One day he plans to count them all, these drawings of the same tower on the same plot of land, with the same number of windows and balconies identically spaced, always the same façade, the same garden to the front and sides of the building, with the same trees, one on either side of the front door. Pablo suspects that if he were to count the bricks drawn freehand on the façade, he would find exactly the same number on each drawing. And for that very reason he doesn't count them – because it scares him to think that this obsessive drawing isn't the product of his own application but of some external force.

His eight-of-an-inch Caran d'Ache pencil goes up and down the page, shading, retouching, and Simó tells himself, yet again, that he will build this tower one day, when he finally decides to leave the Borla and Associates architectural practice. But this isn't the day to make such a decision, and so Pablo tries not to dwell on the fact that he is already forty-five, that this tower gets further every day from being anything more than graphite lines on a sheet of white paper and that a mere two yards from him Marta Horvat is carelessly crossing her legs as though there were nobody sitting opposite to notice.

He notices, of course, though Pablo Simó no longer thinks of Marta in the way he once did. Not that he doesn't want to, but for some time now – and he would rather not remember precisely how long – he hasn't been able to think of her without sudden and even violent interruptions to his pleasurable fantasies. It was different before. He used to dream of Marta all day and in his mind he owned her; he undressed her, he kissed her, touched her – and, since he couldn't foresee ever separating from Laura, Pablo Simó imagined that if his wife died, as all of us shall die one day, Marta Horvat would cease to be simply that woman he undressed in his fantasies and he would try to win her for real.

Two yards from where Pablo is drawing, with a skill that comes as naturally to him as walking, talking or breathing, Marta sits at her own desk, shouting down the telephone at a contractor. She's complaining that this man hasn't finished a cementing job on time; she says she doesn't care about the rain or the two public holidays that fell within that month, much less about the transport workers' strike. She declares, with a vehemence that is all too familiar to Pablo, that she likes people who keep their word. And she cuts him off. Pablo pictures the contractor, left hanging at the other end of the line, reeling from this tongue-lashing and with no chance of a comeback. Without looking up from his drawing, Pablo knows that Marta has risen from her desk and is pacing around the office. He hears each step, hears her light a cigarette, hears her throw the lighter back into her bag and the bag onto a chair. He hears her walking again and, finally, coming over to him. Pablo covers his sketch with other papers; he doesn't want Marta to see what he is doing – not that she hasn't found him drawing this north-facing, eleven-storey tower before, but he wants to be spared her comments about him and his useless obsessions. Mind you, Marta Horvat would never use those words; she wouldn't say "useless obsessions", she would simply say, "The plot ratio doesn't work, Pablo." And even though Pablo doesn't need anyone to tell him what that means, over the years she has often explained it to him, apparently in the belief that Pablo doesn't really grasp how important it is to exploit to the maximum the relationship between a plot's square footage and the number of flats that can be built on it. For that reason, she says, nobody will ever construct a building like the one he has in mind on any plot in Buenos Aires that has enough square feet to build something higher than his whimsical eleven storeys. He always lets Marta say her piece, but Pablo Simó knows her argument would collapse if he pointed out one detail: he doesn't want to build the tower in Buenos Aires. This isn't the city where he aspires to carry out the first project he can really call his own. He knows it too well. There isn't a street he hasn't gone down looking for plots for Borla and Associates, and his exhaustive surveys have taught him that you can't lay a single brick in Buenos Aires without first finding a building and condemning it to annihilation: a car park, a school, a family home, a cinema, a warehouse, a gym – it doesn't matter what, so long as the width and surface area allow for a high-rise. Pablo Simó doesn't want to raise his building on the rubble of something else, but in Argentina's capital there is no longer any alternative. What Marta doesn't realize is that when the day finally comes he'll choose another city. He doesn't yet know which – perhaps somewhere he's never been – but he does know that it will be somewhere where a north-facing building can get the morning sun and be built without anyone shedding tears for what was there before.

Marta pauses behind him. On top of the pile of papers Pablo has used to cover his sketch is the advertisement he has to look at before returning it to the agency. In a few days they are going to start selling another building off-plan and the announcement needs to appear in the weekend's newspapers. The heading they've chosen is "Paradise Exists", in big, colourful typography above a page of text at the bottom of which the same burgundy letters spell out "Borla and Associates". Marta reads it over his shoulder. She suggests he cross out "laundry room" and replace it with "utility room". Pablo isn't sure, but she insists, reminding him that the agency must have used as a template the announcement for the last building they sold, the one in Avenida La Plata, and that while a laundry room is fine for Boedo, it isn't for Palermo. Pablo lets himself be persuaded, crosses out "laundry" and writes "utility" above it. Marta, evidently taking this small intervention as a territorial victory, returns to her desk and packs up for the day.

In fact the day is not over yet, although Borla himself seems to be concluding business, coming out of his office carrying his briefcase and an umbrella that must have been left there on some previous occasion, given that the sky dawned blue over Buenos Aires this morning and stayed blue all day. Borla walks over to Marta's desk and asks some routine questions while taking advantage of his position to peer into her cleavage. She smiles and answers; he lowers his voice and Pablo can't make out what they're saying, but he can see that the bad mood that induced Marta Horvat to shout at the contractor has evaporated. Marta's hands move in the air, accompanying each of her words. Pablo, still at his desk, follows their movement, hypnotized by the red nails; he watches her hands dance in the air, swirling back and forth, making circles, pausing as though ready to swoop and finally covering the face that disappears behind them when Marta bursts out laughing. Borla draws closer and whispers something quickly into her ear, some word that takes no longer to say than it takes him to lean in to her then move away to watch her reaction. And then they both laugh.

All indications are that in a few minutes Pablo will have the office to himself, that he'll proceed as he does every evening, tidying his drawing board and desk, patting his top pocket to be sure that the tape measure is there where it should be and putting his smooth-paged notebook into the inside pocket of his jacket; he'll attach the Caran d'Ache pencil between the second and third buttons of his shirt, with its point tucked in under the fabric, and finally he too will go, after all the others. However, things don't always work out as imagined, and on that evening that Pablo Simó drew, yet again, his eleven-storey tower that will never be built, precisely at the moment that Borla says to Marta, "Want a lift anywhere?" there is a knock at the door and a young woman steps into the room, wearing black trainers, jeans and a white T-shirt, a woman carrying a much larger backpack than you might expect of someone merely popping in, a

11

woman Pablo judges to be no more than twenty-five years old, and without any greeting or preliminaries she says:

"Do any of you know Nelson Jara?"

And at that moment, just as Pablo had always feared might one day come to pass, the world pauses for a fraction of a second before immediately beginning to spin at top speed in the opposite direction. All three of them, without answering the woman or saying anything, without even exchanging glances, feel themselves transported back through time to the night, three years ago, that they swore together never to revisit.

"I'm sorry, but I'm looking for Nelson Jara…" the girl tries again.

Borla is the first to break his trance and ask, "For whom?"

"Nelson Jara," she repeats.

"It doesn't ring a bell," says Borla. Then he asks, "Does the name mean anything to you, Pablo? Do you know of any Nelson Jara?"

Borla waits for the answer they agreed on, but Pablo Simó isn't going to give it. "No, I don't remember" – that's what he's supposed to say, but he says neither that nor anything else. He keeps quiet, following Borla in as far as his silence will take him, yet unable to utter a single word, for all that the other man is fixing him with that particular expression. How can Pablo deny what he knows, and what Marta knows and what Borla knows: that Nelson Jara is dead, buried a few feet beneath the heavy-wear tiles over which the three of them walk every day on their way into or out of the office, under the concrete floor of the parking lot, exactly where they left him that night, three years ago.

2

It takes Borla less than five minutes to get rid of the girl. He says that the name – was it Nelson Jara? – does in fact sound familiar, perhaps because he sold him a flat or contracted him for some job; that if it's important he can look in the files, but if her concrete question is does any of them know anything about this gentleman, then the answer would have to be no. Borla sounds entirely truthful; even Pablo would believe him if he didn't know that he was lying. But the situation isn't quite so simple for Marta, who cracks the knuckles on both hands, making a dry sound as though the bones were literally breaking under the pressure, like the one Pablo kept hearing her make that night, and that sound, or the memory of that sound, heightens his feeling of unease. Then Borla speaks again, directing himself more casually to this girl who has waylaid the end of their working day.

"Now, forgive my asking, but who are you?"

And this time she is the one who seems uncomfortable and unwilling to give an answer that may provoke more questions.

"I just need to find him and sort out some business, that's all."

"It must be important business," Borla says.

"It is to me."

"What sort of business is it?"

"Personal business," she says, indicating by the tone of her voice that she doesn't wish to go into details.

Pablo hears these words, "personal business", and looks up. The girl's hiding something and, although she holds her head high and looks Borla in the eye, Pablo discerns a hesitancy in her movements that shows she didn't come prepared for this barrage of questions. Whereas they have had time in the last three years to prepare. They decided in advance how they would respond to all the possible questions. They tested their answers, they practised in front of mirrors, agreeing among themselves – Marta, Borla and Simó – what they would and wouldn't say.

Borla has successfully turned the tables and now it's evident that the girl is under scrutiny.

"It's personal business," she repeats, picking up her backpack and slinging it over her shoulder. "But if Jara doesn't show up he won't be able to help with it, so thanks anyway." And with no further explanation she opens the door and leaves.

For a few seconds Borla, Marta Horvat and Pablo Simó remain in the same attitudes they had adopted when the girl disappeared through the door, and who knows how much longer they might have stayed in them – but just then the telephone rings and all three jump. Pablo answers. It's Laura, who, giving him no time to say anything, begs him to come home early. He hears a kind of strangled sigh at the other end of the line, as though she were making an effort not to cry. Then she says again:

"Can you get back early, Pablo?"

"I'm always home early, Laura. What's wrong? Why don't you tell me what's happened?"

"I'll tell you when you get here."

"Is it something to do with Francisca again?"

"When you get here, I said."

Laura hangs up. Pablo stares for a moment at the receiver before hanging up himself. He's about to explain the conversation to Borla and Marta when he realizes that they haven't paid the slightest attention to it, that not only do they not care who rang him or what's going on but, also, that they would be irritated to hear any observation not connected to the girl who has just left and what her unexpected presence in their office might signify for the three of them.

"What do we do, Mario?" Marta asks Borla.

"Nothing," he says, and Pablo can't decide whether his assurance is real or feigned. "Don't let's give it a greater significance than it has. The girl came looking for Jara. Jara isn't here and that's all there is to it. These are normal things that happen all the time. We knew it could happen, we've always known. We've been amazingly lucky that for three years nobody came asking for him, right Pablo?"

But Pablo Simó doesn't answer; he doesn't even realize that Borla is speaking to him. He stares at his hands, as he stared at Marta's in the office, though without cracking the knuckles as she did a moment ago. Pablo simply looks at them, turning the palms up and down, opening and closing his fists while he remembers how muddy they got that night, all that earth under his nails, and, above all, the pain – a pain that took a long time to fade and that comes back in damp weather, speaking to him of the thing he cannot forget. Marta, though still shaking, jumps in and answers for him, as if they had been playing cards and Pablo had said "pass".

"I am worried, though…Why did this girl come precisely *here* to look for Jara? What gave her the idea that we might know something?"

"She won't only have come here, Marta," Borla says. "She'll have been asking for him all around the neighbourhood. I bet she'd already been to the café, the butcher, the concierge at his building." And in a final attempt to reassure her he makes a stab at metaphor: "Marta, let's not make a mountain out of a molehill."

His eyes are open wider than usual, and Borla waits to see the effect of this idiom. When neither Marta nor Pablo says anything, he continues:

"Look, I don't think that girl's going to come back asking for Jara, and if she does we'll tell her the same thing – that we don't have a clue where he is."

Borla speaks these last words with a conviction aimed at ending the discussion and, without waiting for any reaction from the others, he takes the initiative: he walks over to Marta, picks up her handbag and hands it to her, helps her to put on her linen jacket and, as she puts her arm through one of the proffered sleeves, says again, with emphasis:

"There's no danger, Marta, don't worry."

Then Borla opens the door and ushers them out of it, switches off the lights – which is usually Pablo's job – and stands waiting for them outside, signalling an end to the working day without a thought for the tumult these actions provoke in Pablo Simó, who finds himself obliged to gather up his things in a hurry and bundle them away without due respect for his usual daily ceremony. Although the tape measure, the pencil and the notebook leave with him, they are not in the places that have so long been assigned to them, and that, Pablo senses, cannot be a good omen.

They leave the office, the three of them walking briskly and talking of interchangeable banalities that could equally concern the unseasonably warm mid-March weather as the fact that the days will soon be getting shorter. They alight

16

on whatever subject will allow them to pretend that the afternoon ended when Borla said to Marta, "Would you like a lift anywhere?", that the door never opened, that there was never a girl in jeans, white T-shirt and black trainers asking fateful questions about Nelson Jara. All they have to do is stroll a few steps to the corner, where Pablo will say goodbye to the others and walk the remaining blocks to the underground station and Marta will get into Borla's car, and each one of them will continue on to wherever they have to go.

3

The underground journey doesn't give Pablo Simó much of a chance to occupy his mind with other thoughts, and as he passes through the intermittent light of stations back into the darkness of the tunnel, he can't help but think of Jara. Since the thoughts are inescapable, he makes an effort at least to picture him alive. Jara entering the office laden with files and papers; Jara choosing the worst moments to be a pain; Jara waiting for him, crouching in the dark passage outside the old office. Jara with his double-entry tables, Jara with his documents highlighted in fluorescent yellow, Jara in his worn suit, Jara and his shoes. They were ugly shoes – he thought as much the first time he saw Jara enter the office carrying a bag full of files, notes and case studies, but he didn't say anything until the afternoon Jara tripped over some rolls of masking tape that Marta had left beside her desk. Helping him to his feet, Pablo was transfixed by those shoes made of rough, unyielding and shapeless leather, with lots of pleats at the toe, like the crimped edge of a pasty. He couldn't help asking:

"Why do you wear those shoes, Señor Jara?"

"Because I have flat feet, *arquitecto*," the man replied.

They didn't look like orthopaedic shoes, though perhaps they were, but leaving aside the pleating and the bad-quality leather, the laces were pulled tight and tied with a double knot, and they were badly polished. Jara had gone to the trouble of applying polish – you could see that – but then hadn't been sufficiently motivated to rub the cloth on the leather and bring out the shine. Even though Pablo is concentrating on shoe care as a way of evoking Jara while he lived, the shoes quickly become a snare, bringing him back again to that night they were worn for the last time. It was Pablo's job to lift Jara by the feet while Borla had him under the arms. And those shoes were the last thing Pablo saw before they let Nelson Jara fall, finally, into what would become his grave.

The sequence of images is interrupted only twice, on the two occasions Pablo has to change from one line to another. It's a short respite, because on the next train the sequence rewinds to the beginning. As he's remembering how his arms felt once they were relieved of that weight, and the muffled sound of Jara's body falling onto damp earth, the train doors open at Castro Barros and Pablo hurries to get out. He takes the stairs two at a time, anxious to breathe the night air; it's later than usual and he knows that Laura is waiting for him with some worry related to their daughter. Even though his arrival will not resolve the problem, at least it will allow Laura to unburden herself on him. But half an hour earlier he broke a Kabbalah: before leaving the office he didn't put his things away according to the usual ritual; he pats his pockets and confirms the absence of his pencil, notebook and tape measure. It's now all the more important not to neglect the other evening ritual – the last coffee of the day at the corner bar, an ordinary bar, a small and unlikely survivor given its proximity to the Las Violetas patisserie at the intersection of Rivadavia and Medrano, but which, in contrast to Las Violetas, Pablo Simó feels to be his own because he doesn't have to share it with tourists and the customers who sometimes make their way here from other parts of Buenos Aires.

He picks a table by the window and stirs sugar into his coffee while attempting another strategy for arriving home without Jara, dead, on his brain – think of Marta instead. Best to focus on what works: that reddish-brown mole that Marta Horvat has on one leg, almost at the point where the curve elides into the knee joint. By the time the spoon has completed several circuits of the coffee cup, his strategy is beginning to work and everything in the world is falling away, apart from that mole and the leg to which it belongs and the woman to whom the leg belongs. He pays for his coffee and walks on home, fighting not to let the mole disappear; in this way Pablo manages to relegate what just happened in the office, the rucksack girl, Borla's lies and Jara's shoes to the status of minor irritations held in some unidentified place from which Marta's mole will not let them escape. He puts his key in the lock, opens the door, and on the other side of it finds Laura, sitting in the living-room armchair, crying.

"I can't take her any more," she says.

And Pablo knows that when his wife says "her" in that tone of voice, she means Francisca.

Her quivering voice is a sure sign that she has been shouting, a lot. Laura tells him that she dropped by the school today, unannounced, to pick their daughter up, but that Francisca wasn't there, nor had she been to any lessons that day, according to the secretary. Then she had gone looking for her and found her in a bar drinking beer with her friend Anita – of all her friends the one Laura likes least – and three guys.

"Three boys," Pablo corrects her.

"Guys," she says again. "One of them even had a beard."

And she says nothing more, just cries and cries from then until dinner time. This isn't the first time Francisca has bunked off school, nor the first time she's drunk beer, nor even, Laura suspects, the first time she's gone out with boys significantly older than herself, but it is the first time her mother has been a witness to these events, and that image – of Francisca hugging her bare legs on the chair, laughing, drinking beer straight from the bottle, passing it to some man, letting another one stroke her knee – is something she cannot transmit to Pablo in any other words than these: I can't take her any more.

Half an hour later the three of them are sitting around the table. They've hardly sat down when the telephone rings. Laura, still red-eyed, looks at them both: first at Pablo, then at Francisca, then at Pablo again. He knows that look, knows it to be his wife's way of declaring, without recourse to speech, that she is not going to be the one to get up and answer the phone. Francisca holds her mother's gaze, to Pablo's dismay, because he knows that it irritates Laura even more. He can detect his wife's annoyance in the tension of her neck muscles, in the way she moves her food around the plate without eating any of it, but above all the anger shows in the blueish vein that stands out on her forehead, just above the left eye. Pablo gets to his feet and goes to answer the phone; he knows that this gesture won't improve the atmosphere, but he doesn't want it worsened by a ringing telephone, left unanswered. Just before he gets to the receiver, it stops ringing anyway.

Pablo returns to his seat and makes an effort at starting a conversation. Hurriedly he tries to think up a subject, but nothing comes as strongly to mind as Marta's mole and Jara's shoes. Further brain-wracking turns up a girl in jeans, white T-shirt and black trainers. He can't talk about any of these things to his wife or daughter so, opting for a blend of truth and fiction, he invents a lie about his underground journey that evening, how the trains stopped between two stations and how the confinement brought on a panic attack in one passenger. He describes the tension on that man's face exactly as he sees it etched now on Laura's face opposite him, but leaving out the blue vein above her left eye because that would give him away. Other details he invents, such as the badly polished shoes, tied with a double knot. He tells how the man even tried to open a window to throw himself out and how several passengers had to hold him back. He resists the temptation to claim to have been one of those passengers – he knows the limits of his own lie – saying instead that they were a man and a girl who had a strange mole on her leg, close to the knee. Pablo Simó tells his story with such gusto that you might think he, and not the man with claustrophobia, was the drama's real protagonist. But neither Laura nor Francisca are interested enough in his anecdote to do more than look up at him occasionally from their plates.

"Pass the salt," says his daughter, and as he does so Laura's eyes fill with tears.

How must his wife have interpreted "pass the salt" for her eyes to well up like that? Or what interpretation has she given to the fact of his passing the salt to his daughter? Pablo Simó doesn't know. The phone rings again and he quickly says to Francisca, "Can you get it?"

As soon as the girl stands up, Laura warns her:

"If it's for you, hang up straight away – you're banned from using the phone for a week."

"Then someone else can answer," says Francisca, sitting down.

Laura shoots Pablo a pleading look. He'd like to oblige her by doing whatever it is her eyes are demanding of him, but he isn't sure exactly what that is. Even though he knows that it isn't to do with him answering the telephone, he moves back his chair and prepares to do just that. The telephone rings twice more then stops. Pablo returns to his seat; the three continue to eat, in silence; for a long time the only sound is the scraping of cutlery against china or water being poured into a glass. Pablo no longer feels able to take up the story of the underground drama and embarking on a new one would seem to be forcing matters too far; he decides that silence is perhaps far better for them all, that for the moment there isn't much more they can do than let time pass; Francisca, however angry it makes her, must stick for several weeks, a month even, to the routine of a normal fifteen-year-old who goes to school every day, succeeds in class, comes home early, and in so doing brings peace to her mother. The normal routine of a normal girl, that is what Laura needs from her daughter; Pablo knows as much because that is how, using exactly that word, Laura referred to her daughter half an hour earlier when she said:

"Is it so hard for her to be normal?"

And he didn't know how to answer because he isn't even exactly sure what it means to be normal. Is he normal himself? As time goes by, will Francisca come to seem more like him or like Laura? He suspects that his daughter won't live up to her mother's expectations, but that by the time the failure becomes evident it will also be irretrievable and Laura will have no option but to accept it. Pablo's immediate task is to get through this time however he can, waiting for Francisca to mature, to pass this age at which children can still be influenced by their parents until finally she leaves behind girlhood and with it the obligation to render accounts of what she drinks, with whom, where and when. After all, has he ever rendered accounts of what he did three years ago? Pablo looks over at his daughter, who's furious but holding her tongue, and wonders if the girl eating opposite him is closer to the one who used to sit on his lap, cuddling him and provoking her mother by whispering "Do you want to marry me?" or to the one who drinks beer in bars and is on the verge of having sex, if she hasn't already, with someone whose name she doesn't even know. He wonders, does he have a right to know the name of the man his daughter will sleep with for the first time? At Francisca's age Pablo and Laura were already going out together, although they didn't have relations until a few years later. At Francisca's age he was happy enough just to feel Laura's tits – that was as far as she'd let him go and it was prize enough. First he would grope them through her clothes with his hands spread like claws, stroking them, squeezing them, weighing them up, and only after a while would he try to put his hand under her top. Laura always stopped him, although she let him rub his face against her chest and kiss it through her clothes as much as he wanted. When Pablo got hard he grabbed Laura's hand and placed it there for her to feel and she, as soon as she had felt it, would send him away, saying:

"Go on, get lost."

And obediently he would go, walking the three blocks that separated his house from Laura's, in a painful stoop, wondering whether to sit on the edge of the pavement until his erection subsided or hurry back to his room to masturbate, and knowing that neither option would be a relief. They must have been fifteen when they touched each other this way, or sixteen at the most, and Pablo wonders how different their behaviour was to his daughter's now. It's one of many questions to which he has no answer.

Pablo glances at Francisca and then at Laura, so distant from each other. He also feels far away. He concludes that the misunderstanding is an inevitable consequence of time's passing, the years on either side of a line that is always moving, a line marking the arrival of one's children at an age in which they cease to be – if ever they were – the consequence of our actions. What would relieve Laura of the weight Francisca signifies for her? If Francisca were either a little girl again or a woman once and for all, if she were firmly on one side or the other of that line. It would be a relief to see his daughter safely on one or other side of the river, and not floundering in the current, which is where she seems to be at the moment, and from where they still entertain notions of being able to save her. Even if that's not altogether possible. Even if nobody is really safe.

Breaking the silence, which he had begun to find almost comfortable, Laura rises from the table, takes her plate to the sink and returns with a bowl of fruit. Pablo selects an apple and bites into it, watching his daughter again; she's not wearing a bra and he can see that her breasts are much smaller than Laura's were at her age. He wonders if they may still grow a bit or if, like Marta, one day she'll buy a pair in the size she wants. Pablo suspects that comparing Francisca's tits with her mother's, or with Marta's, probably isn't politically correct. He tries to change the focus of his attention without letting it return to the events of that terrible night that began when Marta Horvat rang his house in tears. He asks Francisca:

"Not having any fruit?" gesturing with the half-eaten apple.

"May I leave the table?" Francisca replies.

Pablo says nothing. If he says yes Laura will be annoyed, and if he says no his daughter will be annoyed. He opts for silence, pretending to be hindered by a mouthful of apple, then when he's finished that he takes another bite and another, filling his mouth and leaving the question unanswered. She may well deny it, but Marta Horvat's had her tits done – he knows she has. One time she came back from annual leave in a white strappy top and Pablo only had to watch her come in the door to know that she was bringing something extra to the table. That white strappy top showed the edging on her bra and had been made to accommodate an enlargement of about three cup sizes, deforming the word emblazoned across her bust: *Beloved*. He could have printed the word on himself, and not on the fabric of her T-shirt but on Marta's skin itself. It's in the middle of Pablo's reverie about that T-shirt – which he recalls as clearly as if it were in front of him – that the telephone rings for the third time and he, wary of exacerbating the bad atmosphere, automatically gets up. But Francisca, demonstrating that she can do what she likes when she likes – or better, that she will never do what is expected of her – gets there before him.

"It's Booorrrrrrrrrla," says Francisca, rolling the "r" more than seems appropriate to Pablo, given that this particular "r" belongs in the surname of the man who's been paying his salary for nearly twenty years.

He makes his way to the phone with trepidation; it's unusual for Borla to call him at home at this hour, especially with no warning.

"Hello," he says.

Borla kicks off, without preamble:

"I didn't like that girl, what about you?"

"I don't know, I thought you were relaxed about it," Pablo answers, perplexed not only because Borla has called him but because he is asking his opinion.

"I wasn't relaxed at all – I pretended to be for Marta's sake. I don't want her to start panicking, you know what she's like when she's scared," says Borla, calling on a complicity that is also unusual between them.

"May I leave the table?" asks Francisca.

"What worries me is why she came to see us," says Borla, speaking almost at the same time as Pablo's daughter.

"Because she must have been asking all around the neighbourhood – the concierge, the butcher…" says Pablo, repeating the very words Borla had spoken that afternoon.

"Yes, but we're not doormen," Borla interrupts, "and we don't run a butcher's shop. Nobody is the regular customer of an architect's practice. You see what I mean? There's something fishy there, something I don't like, Pablo. I want you to be on your guard. If that girl comes back, find out who she is and what she's after – why she came to the office, and why now, after three years."

"And if she doesn't come back?" asks Pablo.

"So can I leave the table or not?" Francisca asks again.

Pablo sees Laura looking at her without saying anything, then looking at him, and begins to lose the train of what Borla's saying. He sees the blue vein standing out above his wife's left eye and, hoping to defuse the tension, tells his daughter:

"Yes, go on."

The girl gets up. His wife snorts. Borla asks:

"What do you mean, Simó?" as if "Yes, go on" had been intended for him. Pablo skirts the issue by repeating his question:

"What if she doesn't come back?"

"If she doesn't come back there's nothing to worry about – I'm just ringing you in case, so that you can be prepared, that's all," says Borla and ends the conversation as curtly as he had started it.

Pablo stands for a moment with the receiver still in his hand.

"What did he want?" Laura asks.

"Nothing important," he tells her.

"All the same, you could have said to help me clear the table," Laura complains, seamlessly changing the subject and confusing Pablo for the time it takes him to realize that she is referring to Francisca, not Borla.

Laura gets up and takes the dirty plates left on the table over to the sink.

"Leave it, I'll do it," he says.

She accepts, but doesn't want to go to bed before returning to her theme, as if to remind Pablo that if there is going to be an important worry keeping him awake all night, it should be one supplied by her:

"Please – speak to Francisca."

She leaves the room and for a moment he doesn't move, staring at their dirty plates and glasses, the half-cleared table. He wonders what would happen to this household if Laura or Francisca ever found out what he did. Whether they would be able to understand or would condemn him. Whether they would have done the same, in his position. Then he clears away the last things, takes them to the sink and makes a start on the washing-up. He could leave everything in the sink for the woman who comes in the morning to help with housework, but he likes washing, letting the water run in with the soap, watching the bubbles rise on the crockery, rinsing everything and putting it to dry on a dishcloth so nothing slips. The telephone rings again and

Pablo shakes his hands, looks for another dishcloth and, not finding one, dries his hands on the back of his trousers. He answers and this time hears Marta's voice.

"I'm scared, are you?"

For a moment he says nothing, such is the surprise of hearing her. Marta tries again:

"Hello! Are you there, Pablo?"

"Yes, I'm here," he says quickly, fearful that she may cut him off if he doesn't speak.

"Aren't you scared?"

"No, I'm not scared."

"Seriously?"

"I'm not even worried, Marta, and you shouldn't be either," he says, trying to sound convincing. "I really think Borla's right – there's nothing to fear."

While he waits to hear Marta's voice, Pablo reckons that this must be one of the very few times – apart from that night – that she has called him at home for any other reason than to complain about something he has omitted to do, or done wrong. At the very least that girl's appearance in the office that afternoon has served to show that Marta still, occasionally, needs him.

"I can't sleep," she whispers. "I don't know what I'm going to do."

And Pablo wishes he could tell her what comes into his head when she says these words, but he doesn't dare. So he casts about for something else, something less honest but more appropriate.

"There's really no reason you shouldn't go to sleep as normal."

He murmurs two or three more platitudes along these lines and Marta feels better – at least she says she does, thanking him before she hangs up. Pablo puts away the last things, turns off the light and goes to bed. At least that is his intention. When he goes into the bedroom the television is on and Laura seems to be asleep. He fumbles between the sheets for the remote control and switches off the set.

"Don't turn it off, I was watching," she says, pointedly pulling herself up against the headboard.

As Pablo takes off his clothes and gets into bed, Laura asks:

"Have you spoken to Francisca?"

"Not yet," he admits. "I'd rather wait until she's in a better mood."

"In other words, never," she says and then, without trying to make it sound like an order but with sufficient force that Pablo takes it as one:

"Go and meet her out of school tomorrow and speak to her then."

"I will, don't worry about it," he says, and he realizes that this is the second time that evening he has told a woman not to worry.

For a few minutes they lie side by side without speaking. After a time Pablo moves onto his side and strokes her thigh. Laura's first reaction is to tense up, as though fearful. Then she relaxes, in so far as she is ever able to do that. On screen a woman police officer is examining a corpse still warm from a murder. Pablo watches the picture without reading the subtitles. The woman reminds him of Marta, although she doesn't look like her – it's something to do with the way she smiles, the movement of her hair falling over her shoulders. Languorously Pablo runs his hand down the length of his wife's thigh and, although she doesn't move or speak, he takes the fact that she hasn't actively moved her leg away to mean that she's prepared to have sex that night. So he moves in closer, extending his caress beneath the elastic of her pants towards her pubic hair. Laura makes a small movement, like a reflex, closing her legs then yielding again. Pablo bides his time and only after stroking her for a while does he try to kiss her; she turns away but only slightly so that it doesn't seem like an outright rejection, and his kiss ends up grazing her cheek, close to the corner of her mouth. From there, Pablo drops down to her shoulder and there, on his wife's shoulder, he finds Marta's mouth, the mouth of the woman who only a few minutes ago rang him and said:

"I can't get to sleep, I don't know what I'm going to do."

That's why he goes to her house and lies down next to her, stroking her hair until she falls asleep, stroking her face with the back of his hand and just when he thinks that she's asleep, Marta takes his face and guides it towards her mouth – which is right here on Laura's shoulder – and Pablo opens her lips with his. Marta lets him, she doesn't tense up or turn away or close her legs; Pablo's tongue comes up against Marta's teeth, he runs his tongue over them, one by one, because Laura isn't here any more, not her and not her shoulder, just Marta's mouth. Laura has died in some accident, or from an illness – he doesn't know exactly. All he knows is that now he can be with the other woman, the one he desires, and he feels how she makes him hard again as he waits to penetrate her, to be inside her and it's Marta guiding him, wanting him, asking him to sink into her, to fuck her, that's how Marta Horvat asks for it and he likes to hear it, to answer the call and penetrate her as often as she asks for it, just as he penetrates Laura now – not Marta but Laura, who never speaks, or asks, or begs, Laura who has merely lifted up her night-dress and lowered her pants to halfway down her thighs, sufficient for him to find a way in. Laura does her bit, not suspecting that there is another woman in this bed, naked and illuminated by the light from the television set that nobody's watching: it is Marta who moves beneath him, coaxing from Pablo's body something only she knows how to command.

Laura takes a tablet, turns off the light and settles herself into a shape for sleeping, her back to him. Pablo studies his wife; the glow from the television set is enough to highlight her still-youthful shoulder, her lightly tanned skin, the small scar she has always had on her left shoulder blade. Laura makes an involuntary movement, kicking out, as though she is dreaming of falling into a well. He, meanwhile, falls into another, that open footing that was waiting to be filled with cement the next day. Even when he closes his eyes he still sees it in front of him, he can't help it – impossible to make it disappear. But this time he can make the gaping hole in the ground wait in vain for Pablo to do what Borla tells him: to throw the body of a man into it. This time he says no, he will not do it. And Marta doesn't cry, or beg him or tremble. And then, so as not to let the hole remain empty, Pablo dives into it. And he doesn't drop in like a dead weight but floats in the air like a feather, drifting in a limitless, bottomless space, and the endlessness of his fall causes him more anguish because, if Pablo Simó had the choice, he would rather plummet down and be smashed to pieces.

He turns off the television. Minutes go by, perhaps even an hour, and he can't get to sleep. But he must try, he should take advantage of the quiet, the exhaustion of a sated body. Following the curve described by Laura's body, Pablo settles himself behind her in the bed – not touching her this time – and covers his head with the pillow so that the dawn light that will be filtering through the window in a few hours won't waken him. Just as he is about to fall asleep, at that strange point somewhere along the line of fading consciousness, he hears Laura say in a hoarse voice:

"Promise that tomorrow you'll talk to Francisca."

And Pablo promises that he will.

4

Over the following days Pablo hears nothing more about the girl with the rucksack who came looking for Nelson Jara; nor does anyone else at Borla and Associates. Laura's worries about Francisca occupy his mind and, although up until now Pablo's only intervention has been a hurried exchange on the way back from school, one dominated by awkward silences and monosyllables, Laura raises the subject every night, usually when they are in bed, obliging Pablo to contemplate all kinds of possible scenarios, ranging from adolescent mischief to juvenile delinquency.

Until one April morning, when Pablo goes to the estate agency that handles Borla's new builds in order to discuss with the employees various promises that have been made in their name to potential buyers: an extra window some-where completely inappropriate, a dividing wall to be put up because the buyer absolutely must have an extra room, another wall taken down to make a room bigger, a dressing room made into a study or a study made into a dressing room, more sockets, taps where there aren't any pipes, a gas outlet on the balcony... Modifications either suggested by the buyer or included as a condition when the time came to complete the sale, which the seller, under pressure, reck-oned to be "a nuisance, but one the architects can easily accommodate". But even though they use the plural and refer to "the architect*s*", really they mean Pablo Simó, to whom Borla has assigned the task of meeting clients' demands, with the strict instruction that no sale should ever be lost, even if the changes requested contradict the basic rules of architecture, so long as the costs can be transferred to the client and not reduce the profit margin too much.

"I don't know who he thinks he is. See what people are like, Pablo?" Borla said to him the afternoon that a colleague stormed out of the office, slamming the door hard enough to leave his anger in no doubt, after Borla had turned down the offer to collaborate on a project. "Are we running a charity here, or a counselling service? Do we make social architecture? If that were the case, why would I do business with a man like that when I could be building housing estates like we did at the beginning, remember, Pablo?"

And Pablo remembers them very well: the Juan Enrique Martínez estate in Chubut, the Sindicato Textil estate in Paraná, the San Agustín estate with its seventy-two dwellings, in Rio Tercero; projects he came up with, planned and directed. Although that kind of architecture may strike some people as dull, Pablo Simó never turned out cookie-cutter houses; he went to the sites, spent a few days in the neighbourhood, walked around the area and, when possible, interviewed the people who were going to be living in the new development. They were cheap houses, but Pablo juggled the budget to find the best materials and colours. He spent the most time on designing communal areas – the places where residents were going to meet each other after a day's work, where they would play ball games or cards, drink maté and beer, chat, listen to music or watch football, the places where each person would, in their own way, do what all people do at the end of every day: fill time until the new day begins. They had won the National Urbanism Prize for the San Agustín development, eighteen years earlier. Of all the architectural jobs Pablo Simó has done in his career, the social projects are the only times he has really thought about the person who was going to live in the house he was conceiving. And he didn't think of that person in the abstract, but as flesh and blood, with a face, a laugh, a smell all their own. That wasn't the case later on. An era began in which in order to win a tender you had to lower the profit margin by so much that Borla decided it wasn't worth getting involved in that sort of project any longer. Plus there was a revival of fortunes in the private housing sector, along with the growing value of a square foot in Buenos Aires and the availability of cheap credit, factors that meant Borla could make much more money buying a plot and building on it than he ever would attempting some contrivance with overheads and polynomials for the sake of a tendering process that would anyway see him getting paid badly and late. After turning down two consecutive proposals from Pablo, Borla explained to him the company's new work philosophy: from now on they would not think of the person who was going to inhabit this building they were putting up, but of that person's *reasons for buying* what they were offering. A housing development commissioned by the state, or a company or a syndicate, is already sold before the first brick is laid; not so a block of flats. And Pablo Simó, who has worked for Borla since graduating in architecture, accepted his comments without question, demurring only in the time he steals occasionally from his daily work to draw the eleven-storey, north-facing tower. And even when he is drawing the tower he doesn't have any potential resident in mind, other than himself.

Anyway, that April afternoon, on his way back from the estate agency, Pablo stops for a coffee at a branch of a chain that has been scattering identikit cafés throughout the city – quite a different place to the bar he usually frequents at mid-morning, where the same waiters have been toiling for years, shouting their orders over to the bar with enviable brio, and where there are white cloths over the wooden tables and old-fashioned glass sugar-shakers with metal spouts. The main reason Pablo Simó never goes to this particular café is his hatred – a question of principle and loyalty to his belief in sympathetic architecture – of any outlet designed as part of a chain.

"A chain's retail outlets are defined by marketing, not architecture, Simó," Marta Horvat said one afternoon after they had been to San Telmo to evaluate the purchase of an old building with a view to its demolition. They had stopped in front of an anodyne perfume shop that would have looked at home in a shopping mall, but not in that cobbled street.

At any rate, it is unusual for Pablo to take that route, via the corner opposite the underground station, a corner he only ever passes on his way back from the estate agency. And on those occasions he's usually in such a bad mood that he doesn't even feel like stopping for his mid-morning coffee. Today, however, something makes him slow down as he walks past the entrance, then retrace his steps. Perhaps it is because the temperature has dropped suddenly and the unexpected blast of cold weather makes him want something warm. Or because he's assailed by the aroma of recently ground coffee. Or because he feels in better spirits than usual, having managed to deflect three of the estate agents' absurd demands. They looked most put out by his rejections, even though two of the changes they wanted entailed putting windows in supporting walls – something that would certainly have compromised the structure and, ultimately, the stability of the building. It could be for any of these reasons or none of them; Pablo doesn't stop to wonder why, but goes into the café and sits close to the door, at one of those tables everyone avoids because of the inconvenience of making way for customers going in or out. Hardly has he sat down when someone speaks over his shoulder.

"Good morning."

"A large, strong coffee," he replies, without looking round.

But the words are met by a gentle burst of laughter that doesn't sound right even for a waitress in this sort of café. Pablo turns round and finds himself looking at the girl with the rucksack.

"Hello," she says.

He takes a moment to respond.

"Hello."

And he realizes, for the first time, that the rucksack girl is pretty. That's exactly how he thinks it, with those words: "a pretty girl". A man might not look round in the street for such a girl, perhaps she wouldn't even catch his eye – she's not physically exuberant, she doesn't wear make-up, her hair is tied in a ponytail at the nape of her neck. But she's definitely pretty. Pablo can't tell whether the girl is wearing the same clothes as the day he first saw her, but she might as well be: jeans, a T-shirt and trainers. There is something different about her today though; it's as if her face were framed by a brighter light, emphasizing the simple beauty of her features. The girl smiles, more with her eyes than her mouth, and he would be happy to stay like this, studying each element of her face, but he senses that she is disconcerted by his silence and realizes that he will have to say something or the girl will leave.

"Are you still looking for Jara?" he asks.

"No, not any more," she says.

"You sorted out that business matter."

"Yes, luckily."

"And you managed to do it without Jara…" he says.

"Yes. Where can he have got to, eh?"

Pablo doesn't answer because the girl's question has reminded him that she is not only pretty but potentially dangerous, and it is this sense of threat that allows him to reply dishonestly:

"An odd fish. Who knows where he is."

"Fortunately I don't need him any more," she says.

"So how come you're still in the neighbourhood?" asks Pablo, conscious that in a few minutes he will have to brief Borla about this chat.

"I live near here; I've actually moved into the area."

"Oh, that's great," says Pablo, held by her smiling eyes.

There's another awkward silence. The girl pulls the rucksack more squarely onto her shoulder, not because she needs to but as a way of shaping the silence. Pablo is sure that it is the same rucksack as the one she was wearing the other day, though evidently put to a different use today. The afternoon they first met her rucksack was stuffed with things, heavy contents by the look of it: the clasps were straining and there was no give in the canvas, which today looks empty and slack. The girl's face has changed too, but in the opposite way: she looks fresher, her caramel-coloured eyes shining in the young face, her dark hair reflecting the sunlight coming through the window. As if anxious about her appearance, the girl smooths her hair down, pulling the white elastic band on her ponytail tighter. Pablo sees that her hands are red and raw, as if they have been put to some uncustomary work; it's a subtle reminder of how his hands were the night Jara died. The girl notices Pablo looking at them and says:

"That'll teach me to spring clean my new house without rubber gloves." And then, "Anyway, I'd better be off."

"It's nice fixing up a new house…" Pablo says and tries to remember her name before realizing that he has never known it.

"Leonor," she tells him. "And you?"

"Pablo Simó," he says. And he repeats his name simply to have a reason to say the girl's again: "Pablo Simó, Leonor. If there's anything I can help you with, give me a call."

"Well thanks," she says and probes the empty depths of her rucksack for a mobile phone. "Give me your mobile number and I'll put it in my phone."

"I haven't got one," says Pablo.

She stares at him for a moment and then says:

"I don't believe you."

"I don't have a mobile phone, seriously – I don't use them."

Leonor smiles as though she still isn't sure whether to believe him or not, but he takes a paper napkin anyway and writes down his name and number on it. When he gives it to her she says:

"In that case you must be a romantic."

The word "romantic" unsettles Pablo in some way, putting him on his guard; worrying that the consternation may show on his face, he looks for his reflection in the window, which returns only blinding sunlight. He's still lost when she speaks to him, bringing him back to the conversation.

"In fifth form at school we did a modern version of *Romeo and Juliet* as if it were taking place in the twenty-first century. It was all going great until one of the last scenes, when, in the original version, the messenger can't get to Romeo in time to tell him that Juliet has taken a sleeping draught, not poison, and that's what sets up the final tragedy. Do you know what the messenger said in our version?"

Pablo shakes his head. She can't resist the temptation to laugh, her face lighting up for a moment, but she controls herself enough to finish the anecdote.

"He said, 'It looks like Romeo's mobile is out of range.' There were a hundred and fifty people in the auditorium and they all cracked up and kept laughing until the curtain came down. There was no possibility of a tragic finale then. It was a disaster."

Pablo smiles. She smiles too.

"So, shall I send a messenger then?" the girl asks.

"Call me at the office," he says, and he's about to take another napkin to jot down his work number, but she stops him.

"It's fine. I think I've got that one."

Leonor scrolls through the numbers on her screen with a speed Pablo has seen matched only by his daughter, and reads one out aloud, checking it with him.

"Yes, that's the one," he says.

Then she says goodbye, kisses him on the cheek and leaves.

As he fiddles with the paper napkin the girl gave him, Pablo wonders which aspects of their conversation he will relay to Borla, and which not. He can imagine the questions his boss is going to ask, starting with, "Why has the girl has moved into this neighbourhood?" and finishing with, "Why has she got our number on her mobile?" Pablo fears that he won't have the answers for all Borla's questions. For that reason he decides not to name Romeo and Juliet's messenger, and to leave out the last part of their conversation, everything after "Call me if there's anything you need."

5

Pablo Simó and Nelson Jara had first met each other a few weeks before Jara's death, perhaps a month before, and only ever met two or three times subsequently – if you included that last night, when Jara was already dead. Right from the start, though, Pablo had had the strange sensation of knowing the man in greater detail than would usually be gleaned from a handful of short encounters.

It was by no means a conventional introduction. Pablo had been alerted that Jara would be coming to see him at some point, but even so, the man's appearance that morning in the dark corridor of their old office caught him off-guard. Borla and Marta had been talking about him the day before – calling him an "old arsehole" even though Jara couldn't have been much older than Borla himself – after a slanging match in the meeting room. Pablo thought he recognized the tone of the shouting: it was one of Marta's convenient outbursts, during which she started threatening to hand in her notice, saying that this job was sucking the life out of her, that she was leaving, quitting, chucking it in. These outbursts were apt to end as abruptly as they began, once she had extracted from Borla the promise of a week's paid leave in some part of the world with a beach and guaranteed sun all year round, from which Marta would return looking bronzed, with the kind of tan no beach on the Argentine coast bestows on any of the skin types Pablo knows. Locating the white line of a thin strap Marta had not bothered to pull down before letting herself flop onto the sand counts among the most exciting memories Pablo has from all their years working together. The last time was the summer before Jara's death. He almost touched her – so nearly laid his hand on that shoulder left bare by a suggestive halter-neck top. He doesn't know what came over him, can't recall how he came to be so close to her. The last thing he remembers is standing behind her, waiting for Marta to finish with the photocopier so that he could use it, and then a blank, a memory lapse, and by the time he realized what he was doing his index finger was tracing that fine tan line, from the top down, half an inch above her skin, not touching it but following it in the air. Pablo didn't know at that moment whether he was more excited by the image of his finger about to touch her, about to pull at that non-existent strap exposing Marta's naked breast, or by the possibility of her turning round and catching him in the act.

But the tanned skin, the strap's outline on her shoulder, him on the point of touching her, her breasts, the beach where Pablo imagined her – all that was before. Later, only a few months later, there were no more opportunities to let the mind be carried off to such places. That after-noon, after they had finished shouting, Borla and Marta came out of the meeting room and explained to him who Jara was.

"The guy wants us to stop the job on Calle Giribone because of a crack in the wall of his flat," said Borla. "You know how to deal with that sort of stuff, Pablo."

"Just get him off my back," threw in Marta.

Pablo, momentarily distracted by the phrase "get him off my back", missed some of what followed, though he picked up enough to know what the grievance was about. It wasn't the first time somebody had complained because one of their jobs – or work by another architectural practice or construction company – had caused problems in an adjoining building. It was part of the job, another chore, to go and examine the damage and establish whether it was damage as such – a process that was deliberately drawn out so as to win more time to get on with construction and postpone the repairs until project finances were looking healthier – then to minimize the damage and promise to fix it as economically as possible, and not much more.

"The old man's an idiot, a serious pain in the arse," Marta warned him.

"He's bored and looking for entertainment at our expense," said Borla, playing down the size of the problem, probably to soothe Marta.

"He could end up being a piece of work – I can just see it," she insists.

"A piece of work – how?" Pablo asks.

"A piece of shit," Marta replies.

Only a few hours later Pablo Simó met Jara and was able to draw his own conclusions. His first impression wasn't one of the best. As he emerged from the lift and was closing the door, Jara slunk up like a shadow, tapped Pablo on the shoulder and gave him a shock that could have caused a heart attack in someone of a more delicate disposition. In those days Borla and Associates was still on the third floor of a 1950s building and had been since its inception, until the nature of the business, the scale of the models and the need for the office itself to function as a showroom persuaded Borla to reserve a bigger space in the building they were working on at that time, on Calle Giribone – the building where they still are and where the presence of a body buried underneath the basement slabs condemns them to remain. The old practice, where Simó and Jara first met, was a few yards from the intersection of Dorrego and Corrientes, when the neighbourhood was still known to everyone as Chacarita and hadn't yet been upgraded to Palermo. Pablo had come out of the lift into the dark corridor, empty as it was every morning, its smell a mixture of disinfectant and bleach. It was unusual to meet anyone here at this time of day, but there was Jara, smiling, his hand outstretched as he said:

"Did I give you a shock? My name's Nelson Jara, how do you do?"

And although Pablo had indeed been shocked, he shook his head.

"Not at all, don't worry," he said, and showed Jara into the office.

Jara was carrying a plastic bag from some shoe shop, stuffed with files. One of its handles had come off and, as he held it in one hand, the other supported it underneath, so that the weight of papers didn't cause it to collapse altogether. The files, grubby and pointing downwards, bulged out of the top of the bag. Pablo invited Jara to sit down while he prepared for the day's work. He took out his notebook, put it to one side and laid his Caran d'Ache pencil diagonally across it, making sure it fit exactly the contours of the notebook, from bottom to top, left to right. Jara, sitting opposite him, waited, following his movements, nodding sometimes as though approving Pablo Simó's actions, rocking his body very slightly back and forth, though without moving the chair, his legs crossed and his fingers interlaced in his lap.

"How can I help you?" Pablo asked finally.

Jara immediately ceased rocking and started rummaging in his bag, pulling out papers and scattering them across the desk, crashing into Pablo Simó's space like a conquistador taking possession of a town after proving himself the victor in battle. An orange file ended up on top of the notebook, sending the Caran d'Ache pencil rolling from its diagonal while he, powerless in the face of Jara's rampancy, could do no more than follow its course almost to the edge of the desk, less than an inch away from falling to the floor. And although witnessing the displacement of his Caran d'Ache pencil made him feel uncomfortable, Pablo didn't dare move Jara's file and put his pencil back in position, and anyway such an action would be futile: the man still hadn't finished, space had to be found for a photo album, another file stuffed with badly folded newspaper and magazine cuttings, photocopies of municipal edicts and a couple of envelopes ominously entitled "various documents". In spite of the anxiety it caused him, Pablo left everything as Jara set it out: the only thing he removed from under the papers was the gas bill from home, which was due that day and which he mustn't forget to pay.

"Where shall we start, *arquitecto*?" Jara asked.

While waiting for an answer, Jara fixed Pablo with a smile that made him uncomfortable because it seemed so out of place. It reminded him of a door-to-door tie salesman who came to the office once in a while with a suitcase full of different styles, colours and materials. Borla usually bought several and Pablo only one, which he paid for in three instalments. The man sitting opposite wasn't a salesman though, but someone bent on halting the construction of a building on Calle Giribone in the belief that his living-room wall was about to fall down.

"Where would you like to start?" Jara asked again, gesturing at the papers.

And if it had been up to Pablo he wouldn't have started anywhere; if it had been up to him he would have been putting the final touches to a project, planning a new building, drawing one of the many versions of his north-facing, eleven-storey tower, or dreaming about Marta. But he was there, trapped, at least until he could dispatch the chore of dealing with this man; he might as well get it done as quickly as possible, so without making any effort of thought he picked the most obvious answer to the question "Where shall we start?" and replied:

"Let's start at the beginning."

Jara moved his index finger quickly up and down in the air, as if to say, "I get the joke," and began riffling through his own disordered papers, then pulled out a photo album which he laid out on top of everything, open on the first page, and said:

"Here you have all the evidence you need, *arquitecto*. I doubt you'll need much more if you are a specialist in excavations and demolition, as your colleague Borla claims. Colleague or boss?" he asked, as he swivelled the album round and nudged it forwards so that the photograph was facing Pablo.

Pablo didn't answer the question, nor did he immediately take up the album. He was distracted by the reference to Borla and wondered if his boss had in fact described him in those words, as a "specialist in excavations and demolition". If so, he wondered whether the phrase had been without any particular significance, used simply to satisfy a man who demanded attention, or whether it concealed an ironic reference that lay beyond Pablo's understanding. Can someone be an *expert* in excavations and demolitions?

Jara nudged the open album further forwards, landing it in Pablo's line of sight, so that he could now see a series of three photographs showing the same wall traversed by a crack. The wall didn't change in any of the photographs, but the crack did; it was advancing at a rate Pablo estimated at about two inches between one photo and the next. Now he gave the album his full attention, studied the photos and made as if to turn the page:

"May I?"

"Please, feel free, *arquitecto*," Jara answered.

Pablo turned the page to find more pictures of the same wall, the same crack, except in each successive photo the fissure was longer. He could see that this was something significant but, as in a game of brinkmanship, Pablo closed the album, put it to one side and said.

"Anything else?"

Jara, perhaps trying to conceal his disappointment, fixed him for a moment with his salesman's smile and, as though preparing to show him a model even better than the last, made with Indian natural silk and hand-finished, he put the album back into the bag. Then, in what struck Pablo as a deliberate attempt to generate suspense, he slowly opened another of the files where, on an x-and-y-axis graph, a curve had been plotted to represent the growing crack Pablo had just seen photographed. The x stood for the inches covered by the crack's progress across the wall and the y for the time that had elapsed from the moment it first appeared until that day, the very day on which they were meeting for the first time.

"You went to the trouble of measuring it this morning, Señor Jara?" Pablo asked him.

"I measure it every day, *arquitecto*, twice: first at breakfast time and then at night, before I go to bed."

Pablo lifted a hand to touch the measuring tapes in the breast pocket of his jacket and imagined this man – perhaps with a tape similar to his own, perhaps with a yellow oil-cloth one like dressmakers use, the kind that get hopelessly stretched from measuring so many hips and sleeve lengths, or perhaps with the same plastic ruler Pablo guessed Jara used to plot his x and y lines – up on a chair, measuring the extent of the crack as it made its way along the wall of his home.

"Do you need me to show you anything else, or is that enough?" Jara asked.

And even though the image of that old fellow wobbling on a chair made him feel a little for Jara, Pablo didn't forget the objective of this meeting that had obliged him to sit opposite this man, and asked:

"What's the width?"

"The width?" Jara repeated.

"Yes, the width," Pablo said again, with the confidence that comes from knowing you have made a good play: "Señor Jara, you know that this practice will pay to have your wall replastered, but from what my colleague Señor Borla tells me, you aren't satisfied with that, correct?"

"Absolutely correct, it doesn't satisfy me at all. That crack threatens the structure of my house and it appeared the day after you began digging under the adjacent plot of land. Do you know something? It is through that space that the sun enters my house every morning."

"I cannot give you back the sun, Señor Jara; you are lucky to have had it for so many years without anyone building next to you."

"I'm here about the crack, not the sun," the man clarified.

For the first time in their meeting, Jara lost his smile; he seemed to be focussing hard, thinking carefully about his next move. Pablo saw this and made a pre-emptive strike.

"The length of the crack is less important than the width. Perhaps you didn't know that? The crack you've shown me in these photographs is certainly long, but it implies no threat whatsoever to the structure of your house – do you understand?" Pablo waited for a reply, but rather than give one, Jara began once again to rock back and forth. So he continued: "Listen, Señor Borla will be happy to plaster over the crack, whether or not he is responsible, as long as our contractors' work schedules allow it. Please be assured on that count."

But Nelson Jara, far from seeming assured, had begun to sweat. A fat drop was rolling down his forehead.

"No, no, you don't understand me, *arquitecto*. A nice bit of replastering isn't going to do the trick. I know this city's building regulations and under article…" he paused to put on his glasses before reading from a paper highlighted in yellow that he had taken out of another file and now held in front of his eyes, closer than seemed necessary, as if the lenses' magnification factor were not enough. "In Article 5.2.2.6 it states that 'the excavations shall be done in such a way as to ensure the stability of retaining walls and vertical cuts etc. etc., unless a soil survey indicates that underpinning is not necessary.'" When he had finished reading, he pushed his glasses up onto his forehead and looked Pablo straight in the eye, in a way that seemed calculated to intimidate. "However, in the land survey your company presented to the municipality, engineer…" He paused, trying for a moment to bring to mind the elusive name, then, not finding it, was obliged to put on his glasses again to read a fuzzy photocopy that he took out of an envelope bearing the words "Various Documents". "Zanotti, engineer Luis

Zanotti… did not say at any point that underpinning was not necessary and you – I've got all this photocopied – you went ahead with the work, without underpinning and with longer transverse cuts than are permitted."

"Forgive me, Señor Jara," Pablo interrupted, "but what has all this got to do with your crack?"

"Because *my crack* – as you call it, and quite rightly, because it is mine, in my apartment where I sit down to eat opposite it at lunch and dinner every day, where I measure it, take photographs of it, even talk to it – can you believe I sometimes even *speak* to that wall, *arquitecto*?" He waited for a reply but, since Pablo gave none, continued. "My crack, as I was saying, appeared while your people were digging without underpinning. You caused it; the work you were doing caused it. That's all there is to it."

"I wouldn't be so categorical. There are all manner of technical details to take into account," Pablo began, but this time Jara was the one to interrupt.

"The lack of underpinning caused structural collapse, which then set off a series of movements, causing the ground to shift underneath my building," he said. His choice of words and intonation made Jara sound as though he were reciting a report he had made an effort to learn and commit to memory.

"You sound more expert on the subject than I am," Pablo said dryly.

"The circumstances have obliged me to become an expert, and those same circumstances oblige you to offer me something more than the miserable offer of a plastering job. You're going to have to think of something else, *arquitecto*."

With this Jara took off his glasses again, reassumed the smile of a tie salesman and waited. Neither of them moved, each holding the other's gaze while saying nothing – Jara because he was waiting for Simó's proposal, Pablo because he still couldn't think what to say. Then, for want of a better alternative, Pablo Simó said:

"Give me a moment, Señor Jara. I'm just going to the bathroom."

Standing in front of the urinal, watching his piss fall onto the little balls of naphthalene dancing against the white porcelain, Pablo Simó considered his options. It was obvious that this man, owner of the ugliest pair of shoes Pablo had ever seen, had a stronger case than any other aggrieved neighbours he had had to deal with on past jobs. It was also obvious that Jara wouldn't easily be placated, that he was brandishing all this legal terminology with the clear intention of applying pressure – there were other words that Pablo didn't yet dare to think of, "extortion", for example – and obtaining a favourable response to his claim. What he could not yet understand was *what* exactly Nelson Jara wanted. Pablo had already offered to have the wall mended, he could even offer to get it done as soon as possible, but Jara had said nothing about a time frame. "You're going to have to think of something else," was what he had said, and Pablo Simó was particularly struck by those words "something else". He pulled up his zip and went over to the basins. As he washed his hands, he felt displeased by his reflection in the mirror: not by the bags under his eyes – they had been with him for years – nor by the hair, which at this point in the month was too long to be neatly combed and not yet long enough to merit a haircut; it was probably the teeth, which, although Pablo brushed them meticulously, were beginning to look yellowish along their upper edges. He thought grimly that he would have to live with discoloured teeth until the time came to swap them for false ones. He wasn't really sure which feature was most to blame; he just knew that he didn't like what he saw. His hands still wet, he dug his fingers like claws into the quiff that flopped over his face and combed it back off his forehead. The reflection barely changed. With the tip of his index finger he tried to rub his front teeth and incisors, also without improvement. He closed his mouth and thought of speaking to the image looking out of the mirror, except that no words came to mind. The light flickered; suspecting that the bulb was loose, Pablo stretched up onto the balls of his feet to adjust it. An image came to mind of Jara in his flat, balancing on tiptoe like him, up on a chair measuring the crack in his wall. The bulb was hot: it burned his fingertips and he swore aloud. He turned on the tap again, putting his fingers in the stream of cold water. There was knocking at the door and Jara, who must have heard him shout, called from outside.

"Everything all right, *arquitecto*?"

"Yes, yes, I'll be out in a minute," he answered.

"Can I help you with anything?"

"No, thank you," Pablo said.

"You definitely don't need anything?" the man insisted.

"No," Pablo said emphatically, hoping to deter any more questions.

Before closing the tap, he washed his face, rubbing it hard, as he did first thing in the mornings when he was trying to wake up and get Marta out of his head before Laura read her presence in his face. "How does this guy plan to help someone swearing in a lavatory?" he thought.

"Shall we carry on, *arquitecto*?"

Pablo looked up and saw the reflection of Nelson Jara, who was peeping through a gap in the door now, chin resting on the latch, smiling at him.

"I'll just dry my face, then I'm with you," Pablo said, and though he would have liked to add "You could at least let me have a piss on my own," he settled for glaring at the image of the man reflected in the mirror until Jara, whether or not in reaction to Pablo's irritation, closed the door again.

His face was wet and he couldn't bring himself to dry it with the hand-towels Borla always bought, which were as hard as sandpaper – "At least you get a free facelift," he had quipped to Marta once when she complained about it, and she didn't find the joke at all funny. He wondered if the man waiting for him with piles of documents about his cracked wall woke up alone every morning, or if he lived with someone; was there a Señora Jara, or was he a widower? Did he have children, grandchildren even? And although he didn't know the answer he felt sure that, even if he did share his life with someone, for Nelson Jara there was nothing more important in the world than the crack that was gradually opening up his wall and which Pablo had been ordered by Borla to ignore.

Some minutes later, Pablo Simó came out of the lavatory and sat down again at his desk. Jara hardly let him settle into his chair before asking:

"Is an inch enough, *arquitecto*?"

Pablo didn't understand.

"An inch and one-eighth, to be precise," Jara went on. "You asked a moment ago how wide the crack was and I couldn't say. I confess you got me there, *arquitecto*, but now I do know; while you were in the lavatory I took the liberty of calling my building's caretaker, and he went and measured it. Will an inch and one-eighth do?" he repeated, and sat waiting for Pablo's reply with his rictus smile.

"It will do, it will do," Pablo answered, increasingly persuaded that this man would have made an excellent tie salesman.

"Shall we proceed, then, or would you prefer to take some time to evaluate the situation more fully?"

Pablo, who had hoped to dispatch this problem in one day and was quite sure that he couldn't stand to have a second meeting with this specimen, said:

"Look, Señor Jara, as I said earlier, Borla and Associates do not believe that the crack that has appeared in your apartment necessarily has any connection to our work."

"And I say that it has, that your practice is responsible," Jara quickly interjected, but Pablo didn't let himself be cowed by this fighting talk or, if he did, he didn't let it show. Instead he said:

"We have been putting up buildings for years and we've never had a wall fall down. The probability of serious structural damage in your apartment is either extremely low or zero."

Jara laughed, but this time it wasn't a salesman's laugh – it wasn't contained or studied but genuine, nervous and even angry; for the first time this man addressed Pablo by his surname, not by his first name or position.

"Señor Simó, the life of a person like you or me can't be reduced to a question of statistics. A wall only has to fall down once to finish someone off. Or do you have seven lives, like a cat? No, don't kid yourself that you do. You're not understanding me because you don't see what it is that really frightens me. Shall I tell you? It's not being flattened by falling masonry, because that – death, I mean – would be the end of the story and I wouldn't know anything about it. What does scare me is the thought of the wall coming down when I'm not there – do you see? – that today, this afternoon, or some time soon, when I'm on my way home, just about to arrive, as I pass your site, I'll look up to my window, as I always have done for years and, there in the distance, I'll see the chairs around my table, the table itself still with the cloth that covered it this morning at breakfast, and behind that the door through which I enter my home from the fifth-floor landing, my fridge, my boiler, my whole life, *arquitecto*. And you know why I would see those things? Because the wall that covered the little I own wouldn't be there any more, protecting what's mine."

Jara repeated the words "what's mine", then paused for a moment, gazing blankly at the papers he had strewn over the desk until some impulse prompted him to move, imperceptibly at first then gradually faster, and soon he was rocking back and forth in his chair again. Jara seemed to have been set in indefinite motion, but then, as though suddenly remembering something important, he came to an abrupt halt and started looking among the files with renewed enthusiasm, until he alighted on a newspaper cutting that showed a large photograph of a building in which somebody seemed quickly or carelessly to have erased the side wall. It looked like a doll's house, with even the smallest details of the exposed rooms visible. The photograph had the caption "Fatal Collapse".

"You understand me, *arquitecto*, don't you, right? Of course you understand me."

Jara took a handkerchief out of his trouser pocket and dabbed at his forehead with deliberation, repeating the action on both sides. Then he crossed his legs, folded his hands in his lap and once more rocked back and forth in his chair, waiting.

The truth was that Pablo did not entirely understand what Jara wanted, but he decided that the only way to find out was to be as direct as possible. Before saying anything, he retrieved his Caran d'Ache pencil from the edge of the desk, placed it diagonally across his notebook again and tidied up some of the disorder caused by Jara's files – not much, but enough to establish that he was once more in charge of his own domain. Once he felt ready he leant back in his chair, stretched his arms upwards and brought them down behind his neck, interlacing his fingers for support; he looked Jara straight in the eyes and only then did he say:

"So Señor Jara, tell me, what is it you want?"

Just as he had expected, Jara acknowledged the question, but discreetly, without surprise, as though he had been waiting for it. And he was equally direct.

"Money, *arquitecto*," he said. "Money to pay for all the trouble that this is causing me. And all the eventualities. Because if it were just a question of rendering a small crack, I could do that myself without bothering you or your people. But there may be a structural problem here that ends up affecting other apartments too, and my silence has got to be worth something, don't you think?" He didn't wait for an answer to the question. "Money, *arquitecto*, that's what I want: money."

Once again they sized each other up, watching each other in silence. Pablo smiled briefly and nodded, several times, communicating to Jara with this gesture that yes, he finally was beginning to understand.

"And how much would we be talking about?" Simó asked.

"Don't make out like you don't know, *arquitecto*. You're the one who deals with this sort of negotiation, not me. Name a figure, I leave it to your discretion."

But Pablo didn't name a figure or say anything else for the moment. Then Nelson Jara began to put his things away in the bag. He took time over the operation, not in order to stow the papers neatly away, but to maintain the level of tension he had succeeded in creating. Only now that he seemed confident of getting what he was looking for did he offer his hand to Pablo, and as they shook hands he said:

"I'll be waiting for your call, *arquitecto.*"

And then he slid his card onto the table, a white card printed with thick black letters that set out his name and telephone number with a shiny calligraphy in which some letters – the "t" and the "f", for example – extended exaggeratedly high or low in relation to an imaginary base line.

Pablo took the card, read it and was surprised to see that Jara's telephone number shared the same last three digits as his own: two, eight, two. It was a sign that he and Jara, who seemed so different, had something in common. Even if all they shared was those three numbers. He wondered whether it was Kabbalah, fate, chance or coincidence as he put the card into his wallet.

On his feet and loaded down once more with the papers that confirmed the existence of the crack and the validity of his claim, Jara said goodbye, adding:

"I trust you *arquitecto*, I trust that you will know how to put yourself on the right side."

And he left.

6

Only a week after their chance encounter in that café Pablo Simó never usually goes to, Leonor calls him at the Borla studio. He's surprised by this unexpected contact. He had persuaded himself, as a way to forestall disappointment, that their exchange of telephone numbers had been nothing more than a formality, a kind of courtesy. Pablo had told Borla as little as possible about his meeting with Leonor: only that he had run into the girl, that she was living in the area but – and this was what should really matter to the Borla studio – that she was no longer looking for Jara. However, Borla didn't seem completely convinced.

"You didn't ask her why she was looking for him in the first place?"

"There was no need – she's not looking for him any more."

"Ask her anyway, if you see her again," Borla said before closing the subject with one of his favourite maxims, "A warned man counts for two." Then he went, leaving Pablo to ponder what it was like to be a warned man, how much two men would count for and if any two men would count the same as any two others, if he and Jara would count the same as himself and Borla, how much Borla and Jara would count for – and a few other combinations besides.

When he answers the telephone and hears "Hello, Pablo?" he doesn't immediately know who is speaking, just that he has an agreeable sensation, as if this woman's voice evoked some happy memory that has been long buried under the weight of the endlessly repeating days that make up any man's life. It's a voice that seems to leap – like a person leaping from one rock to the next to avoid getting wet while crossing a stream at some shallow point – with a tone that glides from one vowel to the next as though she were reading them off a song-sheet. Pablo knows immediately that this enthusiastic "hello" is entirely different to the "hellos" of any of the other women who might have reason to call him. If he had to hazard where the true difference lay, he would say: this "hello" is *alive*. Very different to Laura's muted "hello", presaging a list of complaints and reminders. Very different to Marta's – a harsh, biting "hello" that has the strange ability to dry the throat not of the person uttering it but of the one hearing it, and which in most cases leaves Pablo speechless, as though even the sound of that five-lettered word confirmed that Marta Horvat wasn't willing to speak to him any more than was strictly necessary. Different, too, to Francisca's "hello", which is sucked in, a prisoner of her mouth, a "hello" weary of giving explanations.

"Hello," he says. "Who's speaking?"

"It's Leonor. Do you remember me?"

Yes, Pablo remembers: the backpack, the jeans, the ponytail secured at the nape of her neck, the smiling, caramel-coloured eyes. And Jara. He had told her to call if she needed anything and for that reason he asks:

"What do you need?"

"Five buildings," Leonor says.

"Five buildings?"

"Well, actually just the front of five buildings."

"What for?"

"To photograph them – didn't I tell you?" the girl says.

She hadn't told him – he is sure of that, he would remember otherwise – and this worries Pablo, though it pleases him, too, that she thinks they spoke for longer than the brief exchange that day in the café that he never usually goes to. Then Leonor explains, apparently in the belief that she is doing so for the second time; she tells him that she is finishing a photography course – "I told you, remember?" – and that when different subjects were proposed for the final practical assignment, she immediately chose "building façades" because she knows a bit about buildings and because she knew that he would be able to help her.

"So can you?" she asks him.

"Yes, I think so. What sort of façades are you looking for?"

"The five that you like best, the city's five most beautiful buildings, according to the architect Pablo Simó."

He stops to think.

"Hello?" she says.

"Yes, still here."

"So which would they be?" Leonor asks again.

"Let me think it over, five buildings with sufficient architectonic merit —"

"Architectonic merit? What's that?"

"Design values, qualities that make them stand out when compared to other buildings."

"No, no," she interrupts, "I'm just looking for the five façades that you *like* best."

"And what value is there in someone liking something?" Pablo asks.

"It's important to me that somebody likes the photos I take," she says.

"That doesn't give them a value. My mother liked the house of an aunt who lived in San Martín and I can assure you that the house was a veritable eyesore."

"But you are not your mother, you are somebody presumed to know about architecture. If these buildings have your approval, that's enough for me."

"It shouldn't be enough, though," Pablo insists. "You shouldn't be content with somebody else's taste. Taste isn't objective – you'd never catch an art critic saying that he *likes* a painting, or a literary critic saying he *likes* a novel."

Pablo feels anxious. He realizes that in his cowardly insistence on precision and objectivity he's in danger of losing an opportunity to see Leonor again. In fact, how much does it really matter what values a building has, what the architectural features are that make it stand out in the middle of a fast-expanding city, or even whether or not he likes it, when set against another chance to see this girl whose voice is dancing down the line? The chance to see Leonor again. But a chance in what sense, exactly? What is he thinking of? Simply of an opportunity to ask the girl those questions Borla wants answered, he tells himself, rescuing his line of thought from its deviant course. The answer placates him and he tells her:

"Very well, if you need five building façades, I shall find you five building façades. I don't know if they will be the ones I like best, but at least they will be worth photographing. Does that sound good?"

"Fantastic. Which would they be, then?"

Her clamour for instant answers takes him aback. He searches his mind as if riffling through a mental card-index, agile fingers flicking through the entries, but whenever the fingers alight on one and pluck it out, the card is blank. Either nothing's written on it, or what was written there has been crossed, torn or rubbed out. So he tries to think of an excuse.

"I'd like to take a bit of time before making my selection. There are too many buildings in Buenos Aires with different virtues" – did he really say virtues? – "and it's not that easy to choose just five. When do you need this by?"

"Well, I have to go out and take the photos by Saturday at the latest, so I haven't got very long to get the project together. I have to hand it in the next week. I think that, so long as you can let me know your favourites by Saturday, there's enough time. Or even better," Leonor says, and then asks in that rock-leaping voice, "Would you like to come with me?"

"Where to?" he asks her, like an idiot.

"To take the photos," she says, laughing.

"I don't know if I'd be able to this Saturday," he says and a picture comes to mind of him and Laura doing their fortnightly shop in the hypermarket where they go every other Saturday. "I'll let you know whether or not I can go with you nearer the time," he says, and he feels something intangible when he says the words "go with you". "Call me the day after tomorrow, and if I can't go along I promise to have the addresses of the five buildings you need ready by then."

"Great," she says.

"Is that a plan, then?" he asks.

There's a brief silence on the line, which worries him.

"Hello?" Pablo says.

"Yes, yes, I'm here," Leonor answers. "I was just thinking."

"What about?"

"Shall I tell you?"

"Yes, of course."

"I was thinking, how odd it is – no?"

"How odd what is?"

"That an architect doesn't know by heart the five buildings in the city he likes best. I mean, straight off, without having to give it so much thought. Doesn't that seem strange to you?"

He says nothing: he doesn't know what it seems to him; he doesn't know what is strange and what is normal. He remembers that only a few days ago – on the very day he met Leonor – he was asking himself the same thing in relation to his daughter and questioning what the word "normal" meant to Laura when applied to Francisca. He's distracted by these thoughts, until the girl's voice brings him back to the present, saying:

"It's unusual – don't tell me it isn't. I thought that I would call you and that you would reel off the five, or ten, or even fifteen buildings that are on that mental list that we all have of our favourite things."

"We all have lists of our favourite things?"

"Yes! You mean you don't?"

"So what is on your list?"

"You want me to tell you?"

"Yes."

"OK. First place: chocolate. Second place: walking without an umbrella in a gentle but persistent drizzle, the kind that stings when it hits your face. You know the kind of drizzle I mean, right?"

"Yes, I think so," Pablo replies, but clearly she plans to explain the drizzle to him anyway:

"It's the kind where, instead of drops of water, it feels as though wet thorns are being thrown at you on a slant. Anyway, that kind of drizzle," she says, and pauses before returning to her theme. "The third place I'm keeping to myself and the fourth —"

"Why are you keeping the third to yourself?" Pablo interrupts.

"Because we've only just met," the girl replies. "When we know each other better, I'll tell you."

Once more Pablo feels enjoyably unsettled, as though Leonor's spiky drizzle were pricking his face. Then she laughs, and that gives him an outlet to let the thorns rush out in pent-up laughter and then to feel calmer. And by the time he's stopped laughing, Pablo Simó has forgotten to ask Leonor about number four on her list of favourite things, because he is still wondering about number three.

"OK, I'll call you the day after tomorrow, then. Bye for now," she says.

"Bye," he says. And he's just about to hang up when he hears Leonor add something else.

"It is odd though – and you're odd. But what should I have expected from a guy who doesn't use a mobile, right?"

Once more, they both laugh.

Once more, Pablo neglects to ask about Nelson Jara.

7

Pablo spends the rest of the day wondering which buildings he is going to choose for Leonor to photograph. It's been a long time since he looked at the city or thought of it in that light, seeking the value that Leonor calls "what you like best". But neither does he look for the values that are closer to meeting his own definition of "architectonic merit". For years Pablo Simó has looked at Buenos Aires purely as a source of what Borla calls business opportunities: reasonably priced plots on which to build; public auctions; municipal land that comes up for sale and which it is feasible to buy thanks to some friend or contact; complicated estates, where the heirs want a quick sale and end up settling for a pittance; divorces that require selling off property ridiculously cheaply so as to separate what can no longer be joined. That's what he looks at these days, because that's what he's been told to look for. He tries to remember a time when he saw things differently, harking back to student days when he could stand in front of a newly discovered building and feel a current pass through his body, an almost sexual sensation, a tension that nowadays he never feels so fervidly, not even in bed. Well, sometimes when he thinks of Marta. Many of the buildings he liked in those days are no longer standing, such as the "paradox" on Calle Maure at Calle Migueletes, where there used to be a house with Le Corbusier pretensions next to a house with Tudor pretensions. At the time Pablo didn't realize how earnest those pretensions were. Tano Barletta, a fellow student throughout his time at the faculty, dubbed them "Chalk and Cheese". And they had argued, Pablo saying that these houses had more value precisely *because* they were next to each other: the contrast forced you to look at them. He spoke to Tano Barletta about "contextualization" – a concept they had just been studying in the faculty and which was surely wrongly applied in this case – and Tano had said again:

"Give them all the contextualization and whatnot you like – they're still chalk and cheese, Pablo."

They used to spend hours walking and arguing: about chalk and cheese, about the city's growth, the new buildings, the old ones. They thought about Buenos Aires with their eyes. They considered whether the eighteenth-century sanitary works building on Avenida Córdoba was enhanced or otherwise by its situation opposite a school with a mirrored façade. They wondered why the Palacio de Tribunales, housing the Supreme Court at the junction of Talcahuano and Tucumán, looked as though it were going to fall down and flatten you. They made a detailed and conscientious analysis of the postgraduate lecturer in Design II, debating whether or not she had the best tits in national architecture. Why didn't they see each other any more? Had one of their arguments gone too far? Something about architecture? Pablo doesn't think so, but he can't remember any more. Try as he might, he cannot recall why he and Tano Barletta stopped seeing each other. It was probably simply that: that they didn't see each other for a while, then began gradually to lose each other, until even their mental pictures of each other were erased. Why did he let the best friend he ever had get rubbed out? Tano Barletta was very funny; he made him laugh a lot. Together Pablo and he were also chalk and cheese. Perhaps that was the reason for their distancing: they were too different and what had started as a joke between them became a wall that neither, in the end, had enough energy to take a run-up to and jump over. But hadn't he, Pablo Simó, been the one who defended "contextualization"? Didn't Pablo Simó have more *value* with Tano Barletta at his side, and vice versa? Or perhaps the problem had been that Laura didn't like his friend. Or that after Francisca was born Pablo hardly had any free time any more and that friendships needed free time to sustain them. Which of his old friendships are still standing? None. The Le Corbusier house and the Tudor house aren't standing either: they got steamrollered, merged together the way copper and tin were combined in the Bronze Age. Is it better to have bronze than copper and tin separately? Is this the marker of some historic advance? Surely it is, though Pablo can't say either way. All he knows is that those two houses were flattened so that the plots could be merged and a twenty-storey apartment block built in their place, with a marble entrance hall, armchairs in some fashionable style and twenty-four-hour security.

He lets Tano Barletta fade away again and returns to Leonor and the buildings he owes her. Not to be distracted from the task, he doesn't let himself dwell on the invitation to accompany her on Saturday. He wracks his brain, trying to remember which were his favourite buildings all those years ago, but of the ones that come to mind he suspects that quite a few will have aged badly. That's definitely the case with some of them, such as the building on Calle Ugarteche close to the junction with Juncal on the even-numbered side, which had once seemed to Pablo Simó like the sole survivor of another age, lost among buildings of an indeterminate period and with no history, and which now looked shabby, tired and old, either because nobody had the energy to preserve what it had once been, or because nobody had managed to obtain an exemption to the rule that forbade demolition for the purpose of building a high-rise on a plot with insufficient square footage.

Pablo jots down, without much conviction, a few addresses in his notebook. He glances at the clock – there's still half an hour before he can shut up shop and go home. Neither Borla nor Marta are likely to come by the office at this time of day. He takes a blank sheet of paper and with a few deft lines summons up his north-facing eleven-storey tower. If this building existed, even outside Buenos Aires, he would take Leonor there and show it to her. He draws the tower the same way as always, with the same bricks, the same windows, the same trees. But this time, when he has finished sketching this building that he knows by heart, Pablo Simó sits looking at it feeling that, although nothing is missing, the drawing is not complete. He presses the top of his pencil to get a little more lead. He looks at it, measures it, pushes it back in with his finger, then presses the pencil top again to release exactly the length of lead with which he likes to work; returning his attention to the drawing board and now with a certainty that surprises him, he draws, for the first time, a man standing beside the much-repeated outline, a freehand representation to show the human scale. Pablo takes a moment to study the relation between the man's height and the building's, to consider how much greater one is than the other, to imagine what this man might be feeling as he stands in front of a brick wall, and finally he asks the question that now seems so obvious: how could he have drawn his tower block so many times, without ever putting a person next to it?

At six o'clock he puts the sketch away, gathers up his things in accordance with his daily ritual and leaves the office. A moment later he'll be underground, changing twice to get to Castro Barros, where he'll step out of the carriage, emerge once more at ground level and go into his usual bar to order the coffee he has every evening before going home. That's all for today. But tomorrow morning, once there is enough natural light, he's going to make good on his promise to Leonor and go out earlier than usual to walk the streets of Buenos Aires. He wants to hold himself to this and not just disappear into the underground, burying himself beneath a city he no longer looks at. Tomorrow he'll walk or take a bus – there must be a bus that follows a direct route across the city from his house to his work instead of describing the peculiar horseshoe around which he travels every day beneath the earth – he will make a journey overland, allowing him to look up and take stock of all that each street has to offer. He will roam from one side of town to the other, like a treasure seeker but with no map or coordinates, with no references or clues, leaving chance to do its work, letting an invisible hand carry him through the city, guiding his determination to rediscover something that, until recently, he didn't even realize he had lost.

8

The first thing Pablo Simó notices on entering his home is Laura's good mood. She's in the sitting room, reading a magazine and drinking a glass of wine. Since when does Laura drink red wine at seven o'clock in the evening?

"Hello, love," she says.

It's even stranger for his wife to call him "love", Pablo thinks, than it is for her to be drinking wine.

"Has something happened?" he asks.

"No, why?"

"No reason – just asking. You look well, relaxed."

"I do feel more relaxed, actually," she agrees. "You know what? I feel that as far as Francisca is concerned, the worst is over. Not that anything in particular has changed. But there are some good signs."

"Such as?"

"I don't know. That she's getting back from school in good time, like we asked her, that she says hello when she comes in, that I haven't heard her complaining recently. I mean, this afternoon, for example, when she got back just now she greeted me so affectionately that I thought she would even have given me a kiss if she hadn't had Anita with her. They came in, they had some milk and then went off to do homework. For the first time in days I felt as if I could breathe properly, Pablo, without that terrible feeling that something awful is going to happen. So I decided to relax and make an effort at being better myself," she says, indicating the glass. "You know what I want to celebrate? That of all the things we have said to Francisca, something has finally got into that head, the seed hasn't been sown in vain."

Pablo tunes out of Laura's monologue for a moment, detained by those words "sown in vain". When might one sow in vain? When the seed isn't going to grow? When there's no need for it to grow? Or when there's no need to sow because one way or another what needs to be born is going to be born? He's not really listening to her, but Pablo notices Laura go to the bar and pour herself another glass and one for him, too.

"Celebrate with me," she says, holding out the wine to him, and as soon as he takes it she clinks glasses and raises hers to him.

Pablo finds himself obliged not only to toast but to drink; he notes with dismay how the wine overwhelms his palate, washing away the taste of the espresso he had only five minutes earlier and which he had hoped would last until the evening meal.

"I'm going to start getting dinner ready," says Laura and walks off to the kitchen with a smile Pablo hasn't seen on her face for a long time.

She seems so happy that if this were another woman and not the one he knows so well, or if the scene that has just been played in front of him were from one of those sitcoms he finds so tedious, he might suspect that his wife had taken a lover. But they aren't TV actors, and Pablo has known Laura for nearly thirty years – how many days does that add up to? He walks to the window holding his wine glass and looks out; the city is lit up for evening and cars are jammed on the avenue in both directions. The glass steams up under his breath. Pablo does the sum in his head, adding a zero to three hundred and sixty-five, then multiplying the three thousand, six hundred and fifty by three: ten thousand nine hundred and fifty days at Laura's side. More, because they met each other at the beginning of February, during a holiday at Villa Gesell where he was staying with Tano Barletta and she with her family. February, March, April and most of May: nearly one hundred and twenty days more. That's eleven thousand and seventy days with the same woman. There were only a few days that could be subtracted, for example, at the beginning of their marriage, when he had sometimes travelled inland, working on social housing projects. Pablo knows every one of Laura's gestures, her different smells; the rhythm of her breathing, which becomes jagged when she's anxious; the blue vein above her left eye that stands out when she's annoyed; her collection of coughs, the spring sneezes, the way she yawns. For that reason Pablo knows with absolute certainty that Laura's head has, until very recently, been entirely occupied by Francisca and her problems, with no room for a lover. Now, on the other hand, now that she's relaxed, drinking wine and smiling, she probably does have space to think of a man, another man. Pablo moves away from the window and sits in the armchair recently vacated by his wife and still conserving her body's warmth; he looks at the glass in his hand and moves it, swilling the wine inside. Would it be reprehensible for Laura, after so many years as a wife, finally to have a lover, if she hasn't had one before? Would it be so terrible for her to meet a man, to have an unexpected, unsought encounter that made her feel that something lost in an inaccessible region of her body could be rekindled? Would it be so bad for his wife to hear, as he heard this afternoon, a voice on the telephone that reminded her of jumping from rock to rock across a river?

Pablo drinks the wine and finds it warm; he has had the glass in his hands too long, swilling the liquid in imperceptible anticlockwise rotations. At that moment Anita walks past, says goodbye and, without pausing, continues to the front door with her awkward gait. Pablo makes as if to get up and see her out, but she doesn't give him a chance, disappearing behind the door which closes with a bang.

The noise makes him shudder and he wonders if Anita's movements have always been so lumbering or whether this is a side-effect of adolescence. He didn't know her when she was a little girl; he's only known her for the last two or three years, since Francisca started secondary school. He puts the wine glass down on the table and goes to his daughter's room. The door is slightly open; he knocks and asks to come in.

"What's up?" Francisca asks.

"Nothing," he says, walking in. "I just wanted to say hello."

"Oh – hello," she says.

"Hello," he says.

From what Pablo sees around him, there are no indications that anyone has been studying here with serious application. Ares, a music-sharing program, is open on the computer. Pablo couldn't put a name to the song coming out of the speakers, though he likes it. There are various nail varnishes on Francisca's desk – one of them black – along with cotton balls soaked in nail varnish remover, dirty glasses and a plate bearing the remains of what appears to have been a sandwich. The window is wide open to noises from the street and blaring car horns. His daughter seems bent on the almost obsessive task of removing varnish from her nails.

"What are you doing? Are you smelling?" she asks.

"Smelling what?" he asks, not understanding.

"I don't know, you tell me. When Mum comes in here she always starts sniffing."

"I'm not Mum," says Pablo staunchly, and he surprises himself with the words that – though inarguably true – seem to renege on an unspoken agreement he and Laura, and doubtless many other couples, have to show a united front where their daughter is concerned. Why should parents need to have their children think that, especially when it comes to education, they always agree? Why not own up to differences of opinion? Why should he not now, here in his daughter's room, dare to tell Francisca that it doesn't bother him as much as it bothers her mother if she has the odd beer and goes out with boys when she feels like it? Pablo doesn't recognize himself in these questions, nor in the questions he asked himself just now about his wife possibly having a lover. He isn't so cowardly as to blame this ambivalence on the effect of wine on an empty stomach. If he were going to let himself get carried away by the wine, he would step out of this room now, go and find his wife and say, "Why not have a fling with a new guy, somebody different to the one you've spent the last eleven thousand and seventy days of your life with? You deserve it, I deserve it." He would say it to her in all sincerity, as though he were speaking to a friend – for aren't they friends? And he wouldn't be jealous. He tries to imagine his wife in the arms of another man and – honestly – he doesn't feel jealous. He doesn't feel anything. Or rather, he does – but what? Relief? If, instead of his wife in those arms, he pictures Marta, he feels excited. Switch Marta for Leonor and he feels furious – he would be capable of tearing her out of this imaginary man's arms. Why, if he hardly even knows her? Why, when this girl has neither Laura's legs nor Marta's tits?

"Did you want anything else?" Francisca asks as she collects up the used cotton balls.

"No, no," he says, and knows it's his cue to leave, but first he asks Francisca, "Are you all right?"

"I am," she says.

"You are?"

"I am," his daughter repeats.

And now he sees that, in stressing "I am" rather than saying simply "Yes", his daughter is also implying that there is someone else who isn't well. *She* is the one who is well. *She*. Pablo waits, but his daughter doesn't ask how he is or say anything else. He moves to leave, then as he's turning the handle thinks better of it and turns to ask her:

"Tell me something, how do you see me?"

"What?" she asks.

"I don't know, I mean – do I look good to you or bad, old or fat, or old-fashioned? How do you see me, Francisca?"

"I don't see you, Dad. You're my father."

"What's that got to do with it?"

"Just that I don't see you; I don't look at you."

"So have a look now, and tell me."

"Are you serious?"

"Very serious."

The girl stops what she is doing to study him; for a moment she even seems preoccupied, as if concerned there might be something wrong with him. But with that fleeting interest typical of adolescents, Francisca is soon back in her own world, transfixed by the computer. He tries again:

"Look at me and tell me, please."

She raises her face. "Are you sure you want to know?"

"Yes," he says.

"Pathetic, Dad."

With, that Francisca turns her back and concentrates on selecting a new song from the interminable list in front of her on the computer.

9

Pablo lies in bed that night considering his daughter's damning verdict. She could have answered his silly question some other way, said he looked old, or out of shape or plain bad. But Francisca chose the word "pathetic". What had he expected her to say? How did he expect her to see him? Had he really wanted her opinion – and if not hers, then whose? He turns over in bed. Laura, who has been asleep for a while, is lying next to him, on the right, as she has for so many years. He wishes he could remember how it had been decreed that he would sleep on the left and she on the right, how they had decided on this division of the marital bed. Did they ever even decide it? Or did it just happen, first one night, then a second, growing into a habit like many others in his marriage? If she woke up, would he dare ask Laura how she sees him? No, he wouldn't – he's definitely not going to ask her. But how does he see Laura? He looks at her and can't immediately think of an answer. Men and women who have spent more than eleven thousand and seventy days together do not ask each other this kind of question, he thinks, and he rolls over to face the other way. He curls up, and in making the movement his body grazes her back, but she sleeps on, heedless of the contact. This would be a good night to wake her up and have sex:

Laura's drunk some wine, she went to bed happy, surely she wouldn't reject him and she might even be a willing participant. The last time he woke her up, putting his hand between her legs, she said, "Is this necessary?", put a pillow over her head and went back to sleep. But she was in a bad mood that day; today would be different, he knows her. Actually, he's the one who doesn't feel like having sex tonight; he should feel like it, he thinks. Shouldn't he? By his calculation they haven't done it for more than a week, nearly ten days. But he can't fool himself: however much he strokes it, going up and down it with his warm hand, his penis is lifeless and seems to want to stay that way. Did the humiliation of Francisca's chosen adjective finish it off? *Pathetic.* He's distracted by a dry rattling on the other side of the window, like bullets striking the glass without breaking it. It's started to rain. Pablo wonders if Leonor will be out enjoying the second on her list of favourite things: wet needles. Or perhaps she's back at home enjoying her third-placed predilection, he thinks, moving restlessly under the sheets. This time Laura also moves in her sleep and settles into an awkward position that makes her breathing come as a light snore. Pablo turns over and pokes her in his usual bid to stop her snoring: it's a short, sharp prod, enough to make her move again without waking her, and thanks to that she stops snoring. If his poking and prodding did wake Laura up, Pablo wouldn't be stupid enough to ask how she sees him. He would try to make love to her, though, even though he's not really in the mood. It would calm him and help him to sleep. But Laura doesn't wake up; Laura doesn't do what he wants her to do, she doesn't go where he wants to take her. Pablo Simó looks at her and wonders where she and he, after so many years, might find a meeting place. It's hard to meet someone you've been

79

with for eleven thousand and seventy days. He's sure they would find each other more easily through sex than through philosophizing about how they see each other, or who they are or who they have ceased to be. How can you talk about these things at the age of forty-five, and who can you ask? How would Pablo Simó like to be seen? How does he even see himself? He remembers that a few hours ago Leonor described him as "odd", and although the word could be taken badly, he didn't mind it and still doesn't, remembering it now. He starts wondering what the girl meant by it and entertains a hope that to her it might mean "different", "exotic" or "unusual", but, at any rate, someone worth getting to know. Somebody special, he thinks, turning over to face the window again. The rain is falling harder now, the drops bigger and heavier than wet needles; lightning illuminates the dark room for an instant and Pablo lies quietly waiting for the thunder that must perforce follow a few seconds after it. It can't not come – that's not in doubt – it's just a question of how long the journey will be. There aren't many things you can be as certain of as thunder, he thinks. Being a special person or not to Leonor, for example, and not merely a "specimen", as Marta Horvat had called him on more than one occasion:

"Simó, what kind of specimen are you?"

And having said it, she used to laugh with those perfect, white teeth that he so often fantasized were biting him. Marta found all kinds of reasons to call him that: because he preferred drawing to managing projects, because he didn't know any fashionable restaurants, because he took his summer holiday in Valeria del Mar, or because he had no interest in subscribing to *Summa* magazine. Pablo accepted the slur and more than once deliberately provoked it with observations he knew would send him straight to the "specimen" category, because it was one of the few ways of getting Marta's attention, however briefly, and of laughing with her.

Odd. Specimen. Pathetic. Hugging his pillow, his gaze still fixed on the window, Pablo places the adjectives in order of degradation. He can think of only one adjective worse than "pathetic" that has been applied to him: "vermin". That adjective would go straight to the top of the list, but nobody said it of him – he chose the epithet for himself. *Vermin.* He doesn't want to think of the word because it will lead to Jara, and Jara, joining forces with Francisca and aided by Laura's snoring – which started again when she changed position – will make sleep an impossibility for Pablo.

He tries thinking instead of Marta, of Marta's teeth, of the mole on Marta's leg; that doesn't work. Then of buildings for Leonor. Then of Marta again. But it's two o'clock in the morning and Jara's winning by a mile. He arranges his pillows against the headboard and sits up. The rain hasn't stopped, although now there is no lightning to help him play his game of certainties. He feels like he needs to get out of bed and go out, walk around a bit, sit in a café and talk to somebody about Nelson Jara. What's this man doing back in the middle of his life? Why now, after three years? If Leonor hadn't appeared, would Jara have continued to be nothing more than a memory that assailed him every so often and then, though troubling, continued on its way? He looks at Laura sleeping by his side and knows that, if he has never yet spoken to her about Jara, he surely never will now. He did speak about it to Marta, a long time ago, but that doesn't count because during that conversation they made a pact of silence that cannot be broken, and because Marta gets in a worse state than he does when anyone mentions Jara. He wonders if he will ever speak to Leonor about Jara and the events of that night. Because he didn't just put him in a pit and bury him; burying Jara was only the inevitable conclusion to a series of prior actions – each of them less significant, but crucial nonetheless – during the course of that night. Will he ever be able to speak to somebody about the sequence of events leading to Jara's death and to his own transformation into vermin? He wouldn't do the same thing today, he knows – promises himself as much, this sleepless night that is quiet but for the noise of water striking the windows like bullets – Pablo Simó swears that he would not do that again. Today he would square up to Borla; Marta's tears on the phone wouldn't be enough to send him rushing out of the house; he wouldn't clean up the scene; he wouldn't keep quiet. What has changed since then? Nothing concrete; what's happened, happened. But now he knows what it feels like to be vermin. Was he always vermin anyway? Was he always destined to become it? Can he ever cease to be it? He wonders if there is something latent about his condition, like a disease written in the genes waiting for the trigger of some chance event. If that's the case, then the disease would have been crouching within him as he moved through life oblivious to it, waiting for the moment to manifest itself, undeniable and brutal, as it did soon after Nelson Jara and he met for the first time at the studio to talk about the crack.

Pablo Simó waited all afternoon for Borla to come, waiting on even past the time he usually left work, and when his boss finally arrived he told him what it was the man wanted: money. Borla was as resolute as Jara had been: he would die before handing over a penny.

"I wouldn't even give that old fart a coin I picked up in the street," he added, calming down a little after the initial fury sparked by Pablo's news. "Why should I give him a single penny? Tell him I already contribute to a charity for hopeless cases."

"The crack looks significant," Pablo observed.

"But his house is not about to fall down. Obviously I'm going to fix his wall, you know that – but I'm not going to let him start dictating terms. I can't stand rip-off artists."

And then, with Pablo still considering the concept of a "rip-off artist", Borla started giving instructions on the way to proceed: that they should keep Jara calm, telling him that he would soon have an answer, and that in the mean time Marta should press on with plans to lay the concrete.

"The only risk here is that Jara goes to the municipality and leans on some jerk to get the work stopped," Borla observed. "Which can also be sorted, you know, but that costs money, and I confess that I'm heartily sick of people dipping into my pockets, Pablo" – and as he said this he put his own hands into his trouser pockets as though there were something to protect there. "Keep him quiet until we've got the cement in; once we've covered the foundations and laid the slab, nobody with half a brain will listen to this loser's gripe."

Marta's job was the easiest: she just had to speed up the work. There was no magical art to that – it was a question of ringing the contractors, demanding longer hours, bulking up the teams, ensuring that everybody was working to maximum effect and praying that it would not rain, as it was raining now, three years later, over Buenos Aires. On that day Marta looked up a weather forecast on the computer, confirmed that no rain was expected all week and committed to having the cement ready in four days. Pablo Simó's part of the deal was quite a bit more involved.

How do you keep a "rip-off artist" like Nelson Jara quiet? Pablo began with the most cowardly of strategies: trying to avoid him until the concrete was ready. But, hoping to pre-empt Jara counter-attacking with one of those surprise visits he liked to make, the following day he sent a note to his house that read:

Dear Señor Jara, we are addressing your concern. In a few days you shall have an answer from us, which we hope will prove satisfactory.

Pablo Simó was gambling on this brief missive being sufficient to stop Jara getting annoyed at the lack of an immediate response and taking his complaint to the municipality, but he knew that it wouldn't stop him indefinitely: a man like Jara wouldn't sit around twiddling his thumbs for long. He would want to see, to ask questions, to hustle, to insist, to negotiate. Pablo didn't feel able to go along with Borla's plan and meet this man face-to-face, knowing that at some moment Jara was bound to sniff out the ruse and see that he was being deceived. For that reason whenever the phone rang Pablo let the call go to answerphone and picked up only once the speaker had identified himself and he could be sure that it wasn't Nelson Jara calling. Jara did in fact leave two messages, which went unanswered, and Pablo reckoned that another two or three calls, which were cut off before anyone spoke, were also from him. And although Pablo Simó was powerless to prevent him dropping into the office at any moment, changing the hours at which he arrived and left – upsetting though he found this upheaval in a day that depended on methodical daily rituals – gave him a certain guarantee against finding Jara stalking him in the corridors.

For all his efforts at avoidance, the same day he sent the note he heard somebody, with a voice that could have been Jara's, shout "Simó" as he was going into the underground. Quickening his step, he plunged into the crowd without turning back to see whether or not Jara was behind him. Another day he thought he saw Jara among the people swarming down the stairs onto the station platform, just as the doors of the carriage in which Pablo was travelling closed and the train moved away – but again, he couldn't be sure. The indisputable encounter occurred two days later, as Pablo was returning from lunch, when he saw Jara standing at the entrance to the building where their architectural practice was, his plastic bag, bulging with files, held on the floor between his legs as he swayed back and forth, the way he had a few days previously as he sat on the other side of Pablo's desk. At the risk of being spotted, Pablo watched him for a time from the opposite corner to where Jara stood vainly waiting for him to arrive: he saw how the man kept checking his watch at minute intervals; how he once more rang the concierge's bell and waited while nobody came to answer the door; how he chewed off the loose skin at the sides of his nails; how he put one hand to his face and rubbed his jaw worriedly. Without seeing it, Pablo could also guess at his furrowed brow, the pain at his waist from standing such a long time, the sweat, the raw skin around his fingernails, the anxiety. Pablo was tempted to cross over the road, stand in front of him and say:

"Don't waste any more time, Jara." He would address him for the first time with the informal "you".

He felt as if he could speak like this to Jara, frankly, as you might speak to a friend, a schoolmate or someone you played football with on the weekends. An equal, that's what he thought, with that word: equal. It was at that precise moment that Jara was waiting for him at the door to the studio, while he spied on him from the other side of the road, that Pablo Simó felt himself and Nelson Jara both to be members of a particular species to which not everyone belonged; two men who had come from the same place and were heading for the same destination. That if every man had a label fixed to some part of his body defining what he will or will never be, he and Jara had the same tag. And this thought, far from troubling him, far from showing him something he didn't want to see, relieved him; it made him feel that he wasn't alone. He had never thought of himself as the equal of Borla or Marta, even though they were colleagues and had all shared an office for twenty years. He wasn't Laura's equal, either: he always had the impression that his wife brought more energy, willingness and effort to the conjugal partnership than he did, and that difference in contribution – it was only fair to recognize it – tipped the scales in her favour. And yet he did, oddly, feel the equal of that man who, rising from the ugliest pair of shoes Pablo had ever seen, rocked back and forth, as though cradling himself, that man who held a bulging plastic bag between his legs, waiting for something that would never arrive, while he spied, like a coward, from the opposite corner. In that place and at that moment, Pablo knew that Jara and he were, in some sense that he couldn't define, the same thing.

And yet, despite that epiphany – or because of it – having seen clearly where each of them belonged, Pablo Simó looked at Nelson Jara once more, as if by way of a farewell; then he turned and went, quickly, almost at a run, with no destination in mind. For a long time he wandered in circles around the city, and once he was sure nobody was following him, he found an excuse to stop off at an estate agency run by people known to him and decided to spend the rest of the afternoon there. It was there, in fact, that Pablo wrote his second note:

Dear Señor Jara, the matter of which you informed us is close to resolution and in a day or two you will have news from us. Please be assured that we will be in touch soon,

Pablo Simó
Borla and Associates Architects

After that he spoke to Marta for confirmation that in less than forty-eight hours cement would be filling the foundations of the building, and only then did he call a courier and hand over the note for delivery to Jara. At that point he knew with the certainty of someone waiting for thunder after a lightning bolt that he, Pablo Simó, was no better than vermin.

He repeats that word "vermin", like a mantra, like someone counting sheep to help themselves get to sleep. And he goes to sleep. And yet, aided by a strange oblivion that is sometimes the mysterious gift of night, not long afterwards he wakes up thinking of Leonor. Or rather, thinking of the buildings he has promised to choose for her. Even in the middle of the night, on the left-hand side of the bed, still listening to the rain on the other side of the window, he's confident that he won't need to look in architectural magazines, or search through those old notes and books from his student days – which, in spite of Laura's complaints, he still keeps stored in the box room – nor does he need to look on the Internet, or to go out blindly searching for buildings around the city. He doesn't know if he dreamt of Leonor, because he can't remember – he doesn't think so – but what's certain

87

is that when he wakes up, having slept a little more than three hours, Pablo opens his eyes before the alarm goes off and passing in front of him like the closing credits of a film is an endless list of buildings in Buenos Aires that are worth looking at. Trying to commit them quickly to memory before they go out of his head, he repeats the names, reciting them under his breath and then quickly jumping out of bed to find his notebook so that he can write them all down. There are far too many, he realizes as he writes – he can't give the girl so many options. Leonor asked only for five. So he crosses out the Kavanagh, the old offices of the *Diario Crítica*, the Obras Sanitarias building on Avenida Córdoba, the Banco Nación and the Olivetti, facing Plaza San Martín; it's not that they don't deserve to be on his list but that, to different degrees, they are emblematic of this city's architecture, buildings that any-one might choose, and he doesn't want to be anyone. He wants to surprise Leonor with options that she may never have heard of. "The buildings in Buenos Aires that the architect Pablo Simó likes best," as she put it.

He underlines, on the other hand, the building designed by the Italian architect Mario Palanti at number 1,900 on Avenida Rivadavia, the art-nouveau façade that so obsessed Tano Barletta on Rivadavia at about 2,000 – or was it 2,100? Virginio Colombo's building on Rivadavia at 3,200 and two by the same architect on Hipólito Yrigoyen at 2,500, one opposite the other. Are they exactly opposite each other? He had better check that this morning on his way to the office; they are only a few blocks from his house and he hasn't looked at them for a long time; he can't even remember how long. He adds to the list the housing complex on Calle La Rioja, designed by architects at the Solsona studio; the rationalist building on Alsina and Entre Ríos – on which side of Entre Ríos, though? – and the Liberty building on Paraguay at 1,300, which he marks with a big asterisk because he suspects it's the one Leonor will like most. The best balcony railings in Buenos Aires are on Avenida Riobamba, close to Arenales; the neat building with the small windows is on Beruti at 3,800. He counts them: one, two, three, plus two more is five, six, seven, eight, plus railings makes nine, ten. He'll have to cross a few more out: he can't give Leonor a list of ten buildings unless he wants to spend all Saturday afternoon with her. Will he go with her on Saturday? He doesn't know yet. Saturday afternoon. He crosses some out anyway. He leaves Palanti, the art nouveau, the three by Colombo which, cheating, he counts as one, plus Liberty and the railings: that's five. A sneaky five, but he reckons that's OK. He draws a line under his list, pulls the page out of his notebook and puts it under his pillow, and then he does manage to sleep a little more. Half an hour later the alarm goes off; Laura's out of bed and having a wash. He gets out his list and looks over it again.

"What are you doing?" Laura asks, coming out of the bathroom wrapped in a towel.

"Looking something over," he tells her.

"What is it?"

"Nothing important, Laura. Last night I wrote down a few ideas to do with work and now I'm crossing out something that doesn't apply."

The explanation seems to satisfy Laura, whose attention shifts to selecting the day's clothes from her wardrobe and laying them out on the bed. Pablo says, without looking at her.

"You may need to go to the supermarket on your own this Saturday. Borla's asked me to go and look at some things."

"Oh, what a shame. I thought we could go to the cinema after we did the shopping. We haven't been for ages."

Pablo wonders why, if they haven't been to the cinema for ages, his wife has to choose precisely this moment to propose it for Saturday.

"Will you get back in time to go to the cinema?" Laura asks, drying her hair with a hand towel.

"I'm not sure," he lies. "Can I let you know this evening?"

"Sure, tell me later. There's no hurry."

She combs her hair, and once all the tangles are out she lets the towel around her body drop and finishes drying herself in front of him: first she lifts one leg onto the bed and dries her calf, her thigh and crotch. Then she does the same with the other leg. Pablo watches her and says:

"You were snoring last night."

Unflinching, towel in hand, she says:

"That's a nice thing to say, isn't it? And well timed! I'm standing naked in front of you and that's the best you can think of?"

"I didn't realize you were naked, Laura," he says, by way of an excuse.

"Well that's even worse! What were you looking at, then? The towel? You don't notice when I'm naked, but you do notice when I'm snoring."

Without waiting for an answer, Laura begins to dress.

"I don't know, Laura," he replies. "I was looking the other way, or I was thinking of something else. I don't know why I remembered just now that you were snoring last night. I just did. Don't analyse it too much. Snoring isn't a capital offence, is it? I snore too, after all."

His wife doesn't answer or even look at him, and Pablo, worried that he's making things worse, says, "I'm tired, Laura. I slept badly."

His fatigue seems not to bother her. She steps into her shoes, checks that she has everything in her bag, puts on a blazer and gets ready to go out, but not before saying to him:

"It's very ungentlemanly, Pablo. I mean, don't worry. I know you and I don't require you to seduce me, but it's just as well you're not at a stage in your life when you need to go out impressing girls, because I don't think you'd know where to start."

She walks out, leaving him alone in the room. The wet towel Laura just used to dry her body lies on the floor at his feet. Pablo picks it up, feels the dampness, smells it. Then he turns and looks at himself in the mirror: he's still in boxers and the T-shirt he uses to sleep in, holding in one hand the list where he scribbled down the addresses of some buildings he hopes to go and see on Saturday with a girl he hardly knows and, in the other hand, his wife's discarded towel; he's unwashed, his hair still ruffled from the previous night, his chin stubbly and his penis – which seemed so moribund a few hours ago – stirring and threatening to emerge from his boxers.

Without moving, he considers his reflection in the mirror. He doesn't put a name on what he sees, he doesn't think of a precise adjective, but he knows exactly what his wife would call him if she could see him.

10

That afternoon Pablo gets his hair cut. Instead of going to his usual barber, he looks for another close to the studio and finds a unisex salon where they assure him that the woman with dry dyed-white hair who's going to see him specializes in men's styles. He is seated beside a customer whose hair is separated into different sections, around which are wrapped foil squares in green, orange or yellow, alternating in an order Pablo supposes may have some aesthetic significance, but which he cannot begin to decode. The woman smells terrible and he guesses that the stink is coming from her head; she's reading a magazine and seems neither surprised nor concerned about her smell or about a man seeing her in this strange and unflattering guise. The stylist suggests Pablo might like a change, asking his permission to find a way of teasing his hair onto his forehead and the back of his neck. Pablo agrees, but the woman has made only one snip before he changes his mind and says:

"Actually, just cut it the way I have it now, but a little more modern."

"Exactly, more modern," the stylist says and continues to wield her scissors as she sees fit.

Ten minutes later the cut is finished, but before drying his hair, the woman sticks claw-like fingers into Pablo's head and gives him a capillary massage. He sees in the mirror how she half-closes her eyes in different ways, depending on the intensity of effort applied to his scalp. She presses and relaxes, presses and relaxes, then makes quick, circular movements with her hands in a symmetrical motion on both sides of his head. The woman leaves Pablo's head for a moment and looks questioningly at him in the mirror; he feels as though something up there – presumably his scalp – is throbbing. Then the stylist repeats the whole process and Pablo feels powerless to prevent her.

"Good, huh?" she asks.

"Yes," Pablo says, with difficulty, his voice shaking to the rhythm of the woman's exertion on his head.

The haircut ends with circular massages on his temples.

"Thank you," the woman says, as though Pablo had given her the massage, not the other way around. Then she gives him a blast of the hairdryer, pouring onto his head some oil which, she assures him, will impart a youth-ful shine to the ends of his hair, and finally she offers to give him a manicure.

"No thanks," Pablo says, without further explanation. But after he has paid the bill he asks, "Do you sell that oil that makes the ends more youthful?" And he buys a pot of that.

After the hairdresser, he goes to buy clothes. He wants jeans and a new sweater. When was the last time he bought his own clothes? Everything he's had in the last few years was bought by Laura: socks, shirts, trousers, pants, T-shirts, sweaters, swimming trunks, even the suit that has rarely been used and hangs in the wardrobe in his room. Laura insisted on Pablo buying a suit for the fifteenth birthday of the daughter of a cousin they hadn't seen for years and won't see again until the girl gets married. Pablo buys only his shoes for himself because Laura never gets the size exactly right. It's as though Pablo's feet, after so many years of marriage, are the only part of his body he has managed to keep to himself.

The sales assistant pulls out some sweaters to show him. Pablo says:

"Nothing on the grey spectrum, or beige or blue."

He could swear that in his own wardrobe there have never been sweaters in any other colour. Beige for Pablo Simó is a "residents' association" colour – the colour of consensus; when there are as many opinions on what colour to paint a landing as there are apartments, inevitably the default choice is a shade of beige: dark, light, milky tea, *café au lait*, maté. Once a client assured him that there was a tone called "Mediterranean beige", which Pablo never managed to find in the catalogue of any paint shop in Buenos Aires. He remembers that Borla told him:

"Make her up a sample of shitty beige – I'm sure it will do the trick."

And Pablo doesn't remember if it did, but whenever he gets a new colour chart he looks among the beiges to see if anyone has yet dared call "shitty" by its name. So not beige, because it's a consensus colour, and not those blues and greys that Pablo associates with large groups of people: the mass of commuters coming out of the underground at rush hour, or marchers on a demonstration; even the fans who fill the stands at a football match – if the eye were capable of separating out the flags and football strips, blue and grey would predominate. For that reason Pablo repeats to the assistant, while she looks on the shelf for his size in each of the available styles:

"Not beige, grey or blue."

"Yes, yes," she says, turning to him with a pile of garments.

Pablo rules out a pink sweater, another in lilac and one in red, without commentary (after all, he was the one that requested different colours) and takes to the changing room a yellow one that is neither "canary" nor too strident, with a zipper at the front instead of buttons, as well as one in mint green in a soft, fine wool he has only to touch to know it must be worth a fortune. Since when has he known so much about colours not destined to paint a wall? When he was a boy they had even thought he might be colour-blind because he made everything brown so as to avoid sharpening the other pencils.

"Cardigans are very popular at the moment," the sales assistant says, approving his selection.

She suggests he start trying on the sweaters he has already chosen, while she looks out two or three styles of jeans "that would be right for you". The words stir in him a fear that this girl may be seeing him a certain way – old, dated, pathetic? – but the fear turns out to be unfounded because she comes back a few minutes later with three models, one classic and the other two full of slashes and pockets. These Pablo rejects without even trying them on. The first pair he does try, and knows instantly that Laura will disapprove of them. They can be as classic as they like, but the jeans he sees in the mirror are of an indigo that is almost black and his wife believes – and at an end-of-year office party she even argued this point with Marta Horvat, who disagreed – that on building sites the dust that is raised before the cement goes down shows much more on a dark background than on a light one. When she sees these, Laura will say something along those lines, even though he no longer visits sites pre-cement. There's no need, that's not his job: he is a designer, draughtsman, administrator, responsible for any of the studio jobs not specifically assigned to someone else in the team. For that reason he avoids the cement without feeling the need for explanations; just as he avoids, whenever he has notice of it, any other situation that might cause him to revisit – as a pair of simple dark jeans has caused him to now – the open footing waiting to be cemented, where Jara's body is trapped forever.

Even though in those days it wasn't his job to do it, and nobody had asked it of him, the afternoon before Jara's death Pablo Simó had dropped in on the site in Calle Giribone. It was probably because he wanted to see Marta, who hadn't been at the office for days. Or because he wanted to confirm, with his own eyes, that the pit would be cemented over the next day and that he, vermin or otherwise, would no longer have to worry about Jara. Perhaps it was fate that led him there and placed him on that stage to be a witness. He can't remember any more the real reason, only that he was there that afternoon. Everyone was working on schedule, making the final necessary arrangements before the cement was poured in the following day: the open footings at base level; the reinforcement bars in position in each column and bent to the degree specified in the plans; the area clear so that, when the cement mixer arrived the next morning, the truck would have a clear path to the point at which the mixture had to be tipped; the on-site team instructed in the procedure for the following day. Marta was surprised to see him:

"What are you doing here, Pablo? Is something up?"

"No, nothing. I need to visit a site a few blocks from here," he lied, "so I thought I'd drop in to see if everything was OK or if you needed anything."

"For this to be over – that's what I need," she said, and turned her attention to the shuttering of a beam.

Marta looked tired, but she still seemed even prettier to Pablo than when she was dressed as an executive for the office: her trousers tucked into low-heeled boots, a long, tight polo neck that emphasized her waist, hips and breasts. An outfit doubtless chosen to allow free movement on irregular terrain without sacrificing that sensuality that Marta liked to flaunt, even in a place like this, full of men who didn't mind eyeing her up even if she was their boss, and clearly they had no qualms about it that day as they boldly ran their eyes over her, even when Pablo stood glowering next to Marta Horvat, as though he enjoyed sole rights to this woman. Marta went to speak to the foreman; from where Pablo was standing, it looked as though they were going over a task list together, checking that everything was going according to plan. The man showed her some forms, which she read and signed with a ballpoint pen – blue? – every so often holding it between her teeth. When she had finished with the forms, Marta returned to where Pablo was standing, took him by the arm and led him behind a wall of hollow bricks that had been piled up near the party wall.

"Come, I want to tell you something," she said.

The confined space forced a proximity on them that made Pablo nervous, as it always did to have Marta so close.

"He's spent the whole day watching."

"Who?" Pablo asked.

"Jara. He stood there, behind the fence, next to the site board, and looked right inside, cool as a cucumber. Nothing fazes that guy. He made notes in a file and took photographs; I sent the foreman over to tell him that taking photographs of the work wasn't permitted and to frighten him a bit. He spoke to Jara for about ten minutes, but it made no difference – he didn't care. He said that the street is public and that if we didn't like him watching, it must be because we had something to hide, 'a dirty arse', he said. 'Dirty arse'," repeated Marta. "I wouldn't like to know what that old man's arse smells like. He was here for nearly an hour, taking folders out of his bag and putting them in again; I don't know what he was up to – reading, making notes, all rubbish, I expect. What else would you expect from a man like that? The foreman said he even tried talking to him about football – that got rid of him. Have you got a cigarette?"

Pablo took a moment to answer because he was thinking that, although he had never liked women swearing, hearing Marta say "dirty arse" made him feel mildly excited. She patted his jacket pockets, feeling for a cigarette packet, first the breast pocket and then the sides. Only when she had finished touching him did Pablo say, "I don't smoke, Marta."

"Right," she said. "I'll go and ask the boys."

And off she went. Pablo followed her with his eyes and so did the other men; it seemed to him that some of them even stopped or at least slowed their work as she walked past. Finally someone offered her a packet and she took a cigarette, lifting it to her mouth; the foreman stepped forward with a lighter and lit it for her. Marta inhaled and blew out hard – harder than necessary, Pablo thought – as if hoping to expel all the tensions of the day in a puff. Somebody rolled a tin drum over to her and turned it on its end, offering it as a seat. One of the workmen must have made a joke, because Marta laughed, then she said something and laughed again, the men who had gathered around her laughing too. Marta Horvat gestured with her hand for him to join them. Pablo walked over to the group and stood as close to Marta as he could. As he had thought, they were telling jokes. A playful duel was taking place between a builder from Córdoba and a pitman from

Tucumán who they called "King Mole" and who headed the team that had excavated the base level and opened the footings ready to receive the cement. Pablo thought the duel would be won by King Mole, whose years digging earth had given him strong arms and who was very funny besides. He would have been happy to listen to King Mole tell his jokes, but Pablo's eyes were drawn to the side wall of Jara's building and he couldn't help counting the floors to the level he guessed must be his. He stood staring at that window which, as so often, had been opened up in the wall in contravention of building regulations. If he had realized before that Jara's apartment had an unauthorized window, he would have used that argument to reverse the burden of proof and assure the man that the true cause of his crack was there, in his illegal window. But he doesn't need any new arguments now. Tomorrow it will all be over. The side wall was dirty, like the rest of the building, and from where he was standing it was impossible to distinguish the crack. But Pablo Simó could imagine it. Just as he imagined each of the things that Jara had described to him: the table, chairs, the fridge, the boiler, his markings on the wall. And Jara, too, spying on them from behind the curtain, wondering why they were laughing, as though no one ought to laugh at such a short distance from his wounded wall. Pablo looked down and spotted the glowing butt of the cigarette Marta had smoked and was now stamping on with the toe of her boot, grinding it until it was out.

"Shall we press on?" said Marta Horvat to her workmen.

And everyone got back to work.

As time went on, despite her tiredness, Marta seemed calmer – more so than Pablo had seen her since Jara entered their lives.

"You look well," he told her.

"Because it's done, Pablo. Look at the time. It's too late now for that arsehole to do anything to stop the work, nobody can hear his complaint now, no inspector can turn up unannounced. Tomorrow at eight o'clock in the morning the pit goes, and the old man goes with it."

That's what she said that afternoon, "the pit goes and the old man goes," and today, when Pablo looks back, he wonders if Marta Horvat has ever recognized the prophetic quality of those words, which were said in passing, as we say so many things in our lives, without really thinking about the weight of our words.

But as Pablo Simó would soon find out, Nelson Jara had not, after all, been hiding behind his curtain spying on the work at Calle Giribone. That afternoon, after visiting Marta, Pablo took the underground back home as he did every day, journeying beneath the earth, following his usual long route with its several changes of line. Emerging onto the street at Castro Barros, he heard again the cry of "Simó" that a few days earlier he had attributed to Jara. This time, however, he didn't panic or rush to get away: given the impossibility of meeting Jara only two blocks from his own home, the cry had to have come from someone else. Only when he turned to look over his shoulder did he see that he was wrong: there was Jara, running across the road to catch up with him and clearly agitated.

"What are you doing here?" Pablo asked him, almost rudely.

"Waiting for you. What else might I be doing so far from my own stamping ground, *arquitecto*?"

"But how did you know you would find me on this particular corner?"

"It wasn't the corner I identified but the station. Two plus two is four, *arquitecto*. You come out of the underground every morning and go back into it every afternoon. The day we met at your office I saw the gas bill on your desk, and Castro Barros is the closest station to the address that was on that bill, so I found a bar from which to watch this exit – and I waited. Did you know that if you got out in Medrano and walked seven or eight blocks you'd avoid so many changes?"

"I don't like walking."

"What a mistake you're making; it's good to walk. I walk a lot."

Pablo would have liked to say, "And what do I care?", but he wasn't given to ripostes, not even when he was angry, as he was that afternoon.

"I took a gamble," Jara went on, "because the bill wasn't in your name but in the name of a woman. Your wife – or somebody else, *arquitecto*?"

Pablo stared at him without managing to formulate a response, and Jara continued: "But you're not the sort of man to pay another woman's gas bill – correct me if I'm wrong?"

For all his carefully chosen words, his irony, his apparent mastery of the situation, Jara appeared rather tense.

"Shall we have a coffee in Las Violetas?" he suggested, and although this was phrased as a question, Pablo had the impression that saying no wasn't an option. Instead he replied with another question, somewhat out of sync, but in keeping with the strange rhythm of this absurd conversation.

"Did you really examine my gas bill?"

"Don't take offence or draw the wrong conclusions," Jara said as they crossed back over the road and entered the café. "Shall I tell you why I looked at it? I have an obsession with the money spent on services in this city – it's an outrage – and I'm always comparing what I spend with what other people are spending. And your bill was right there. You were taking a long time in the bathroom and I was waiting for you, staring mindlessly at your desk, not meaning to pry, but my eyes fell on it – and it wasn't even in an envelope. All I did was move it a little and have a look. Do you see what I mean?"

"I am trying to, Jara," said Pablo, and he said nothing more, hoping not to open further avenues of conversation that he would surely regret.

They didn't speak again until the waiter came and both of them ordered a coffee.

"You're spending too much on gas, *arquitecto* – you don't think you might have a leak?"

"I don't think so. I would have smelled something."

"Sometimes they are very small and the smell gets lost among the other household smells, or it dissipates if there is plenty of ventilation. I would get it looked at – although there are three of you, so you're using more than a single man."

"How do you know that there are three of us?"

"Didn't you tell me yourself, *arquitecto*?"

"Not that I remember."

"I think you must have. Otherwise how would I know? It's not mentioned on the bill."

"Of course it's not mentioned on the bill," Pablo repeated with irritation and a creeping unease.

"You're not thinking that I go around spying on you?"

"I'm not thinking anything, Jara."

"You think more than you let on."

The waiter brought their coffees and a jug of milk nobody had asked for, and after he had gone Jara said:

"You must have told me yourself; don't give it another thought."

Without taking his eyes off Pablo, Nelson Jara drank his coffee in little measured sips. Pablo waited as long as he could, and when he couldn't bear it any more he said:

"What do you want, Jara? Didn't you get my notes?"

"Yes, I got them, but at this stage in the game I don't know how much faith to put in one of your notes. To believe you, I needed to see your face."

"What are you trying to insinuate?"

"Insinuate, nothing; simply to convey my concern, my annoyance, even I would say my bitter certainty that something round here smells bad. In the last days there have been strange comings and goings at the site, or rather, not exactly strange, but more hurried, to be concrete, as if they were trying to get something done sooner than planned and someone had put the screws on them."

"And why does that alarm you?"

"Because I'm frightened that in the end the screws will be on me."

"If the work is over sooner, that's going to be better for you —", Pablo began to say, to reassure him, but Jara shrugged his shoulders:

"I don't give a damn if they finish the work early; the only thing I care about is getting fair compensation, and you wrote in those notes – to which you put your signature – that your office was studying my case."

"We are studying it; I just don't have a firm answer for you yet."

"And once the foundations are covered it will be too late for answers. Look, Simó, I may seem like an idiot, but I'm not, and when people treat me like one I get very annoyed, I get very bad. I mean seriously bad."

Jara rubbed his hands over his face, up and down, hard, as though trying to wake himself from a dream, then he looked around him and paused just long enough to take a deep breath and calm his uneven breathing. Then he went back in for the kill:

"All you've done is make *me* lose time in order to give it to others," Jara said, looking him straight in the eye, and this time Pablo couldn't hold his gaze. "Or am I wrong?" he added, and thumped the table so that the cups jangled on their saucers and customers sitting at a neighbouring table turned to look at them. "Always the same," he said, and stopped himself just before making a second strike, his clenched fist in the air as if he were thumping some non-existent thing. "Always the same story, Simó," Jara repeated and stood up to leave, but Pablo stopped him:

"What do you mean by 'always the same', Jara?"

"That the little fish, instead of looking after their own, always end up defending the interests of the big fish. Take a look at the history of humanity and see if I'm wrong. And you know why they do it? To flatter themselves that they can become something they aren't. Simó, no matter how much you put yourself on their side, you're never going to be one of them – do you understand?"

And Pablo, silent opposite Jara, understood, understood all too well and knew himself to be vermin. But the epiphany wasn't enough to persuade him that he – Pablo Simó, unaided – might choose this moment to change the course of humanity. Jara, after waiting in silence for a moment, seemed to see that.

"At least pay for my coffee," he said, standing up, and he left.

The afternoon, the encounter and this unpleasant episode appeared to be over, yet Pablo felt even more troubled than he had when Jara was sitting across the table from him. He stayed sitting in Las Violetas for a while, staring at the famous stained-glass dome that crowned that corner of the street, not even noticing the imagery on it, but dazed by the clatter of teaspoons on crockery all around him. And he waited. He was scared to leave and find Jara still prowling around outside; knowing him, it was possible. In fact, at the very moment Pablo turned and gestured to the waiter to bring his bill, Nelson Jara burst back in through the door and walked with determination towards his table. He seemed very out of breath.

"Just one more thing, Simó – an architectonic query, if you'll allow me. Is there any thing, any circumstance, any strange happening that could halt the cement tomorrow?"

"Rain," Pablo answered automatically, almost without thinking.

Jara stared at him, nodding as a light smile appeared on his face. "So, if it has to rain, it will rain. Make no mistake: it's going to rain, Simó," he said. And this time, when he left, he didn't come back.

It would be a shame if it rained on Saturday, the day he's going out with Leonor, Pablo thinks as the sales assistant rings up his dark jeans and his yellow cardigan. Though perhaps "going out" isn't really the right way to put it. They're going on a stroll, an excursion, an architectural tour, a photographic safari. He settles on "tour", plain and simple, while tucking his credit card back into his wallet; it would be a shame to make their tour in the rain, unless it was that kind of drizzle that comes second on Leonor's list of favourite things.

Or unless – and this would be even better – he plucked up the courage to ask her what number three was. And she told him.

11

At the very moment that Pablo is pulling up the zipper of his yellow cardigan, Laura comes into the bedroom.

"And this?" she asks.

"And this what?" he says.

His wife nods at the sweater.

"I bought it the other day. I saw it in a shop window near the office. I needed a lightweight jacket," he offers, by way of justification.

"A little zip-up," she says.

"Isn't it what the English call a 'cardigan'?" Pablo asks.

"I don't know – it doesn't matter," Laura replies. "But you don't need to go buying the first one you see. You could have told me and I would have looked for one for you."

"You don't like it."

"No – yes – it's not ugly," she says. "I just don't know if it's your style."

"Why not?" Pablo probes.

"Other things suit you better," Laura says.

"What suits me better?"

"It's fine – ignore me. What counts is that you like it," his wife says and adds, as though drawing a line under this exchange, "I'm going to the supermarket now, so remember that if you finish early we can go to the cinema."

But Pablo insists:

"Why do you say it isn't my style?"

"Did I say that?" Laura asks, picking up her bag and taking her winter jacket off a hanger.

"Yes, you said it wasn't my style."

"I didn't say that."

"But you said it just a minute ago!"

"I said that I didn't *know* if it was your style, not that it wasn't."

"And there's a difference?"

"Are you trying to pick a fight? You see – that's not your style either."

Laura puts on her jacket. Her hair gets caught under the jacket collar and she rearranges it in front of the mirror.

"Perhaps my style is changing," he says.

Laura looks at him but says nothing. Then Pablo adds, "I bought these jeans too," pulling up his jeans from the waistband, tugging at them a little as though to suggest that he could fill them better. "Do you like them?"

She studies Pablo's reflection in the mirror and says:

"Try not to go anywhere very dusty – dark jeans are impossible to clean."

"Yes, don't worry," says Pablo Simó, giving his wife a kiss. He picks up the list of buildings for Leonor that was lying on the bed with his wallet, puts both of these in his pocket and leaves the room before Laura.

He's arranged to meet Leonor at the corner of Rivadavia and Callao. Even though most of the buildings selected for this tour are in the danger zone because of their proximity to his house, Pablo knows that Laura's route to the supermarket will take her in the direction of the Flores district, not towards the centre, like him. By the time Pablo arrives with Leonor at Rivadavia 3,200, their furthest point on this avenue, his wife will be safely far away. Glancing at his watch, he sees that he has arrived twenty-five minutes early. He looks over at the El Molino café, closed in 1997 and seemingly doomed to remain closed; the National Congress building; the bar on the opposite corner, across Callao; beyond it the Plaza de los Dos Congresos is thronged with flags and banners making demands Pablo can't quite make out. He sees a small, grubby tent – not part of today's protest, he decides, but left over from some previous demonstration. He wonders at which of the four cardinal points Leonor will appear. So as not to spend too long waiting on this corner, he walks up the Avenida Rivadavia, looking for a quiet bar where he can wait for the girl away from the clamour of a protest that doesn't interest him. Ought he to be interested? Not today, he tells himself, not on the day he's going out for the first time with a girl – though strictly speaking this isn't "going out" – after eleven thousand and seventy days of monogamy.

He finds a suitable bar, goes in, picks a table and sits down. Then he takes the list of buildings out of his pocket, lays it on the table and goes over it again. The selection now strikes him as worryingly flawed: it's a century out of date. Most of the buildings he has picked for Leonor were built nearly a hundred years ago. Since when has he been so interested in art nouveau? Why hasn't he chosen a single modern tower? Why, instead of walking the girl around Rivadavia, didn't he propose a tour that takes in, for example, the new waterfront developments at Puerto Madero or the business district of Catalinas, both abounding in prize-winning, celebrated architecture from the last decades which he could have shown and explained to her, flaunting his expertise? Why didn't he think of taking her to Palermo Soho, or Palermo Hollywood, or Palermo

Queens, even to Las Cañitas – not the home of his favourite architecture, but still a perfectly pleasant place to walk with a girl like Leonor? All this he asks himself while sitting in a bar poorly lit by thick amber-coloured globes speckled with air-bubbles, and with bare Formica tables, hard wooden chairs, white plastic napkin rings (prism-shaped), and old dispensers with advertisements for vermouth stamped on them in red; it's a Saturday afternoon and the place is empty apart from himself, the waiter and the cashier.

He looks in his pocket and realizes that he isn't carrying his Caran d'Ache pencil, or his measuring tape. He asks the waiter for a pen and writes an *A* and an *N* beside the building at Rivadavia 2,000 that is definitely art nouveau; another *AN* goes beside the building designed by Palanti. Pablo knows that even Colombo's buildings are classed within the same movement, although for Tano Barletta – with whom he had argued for two whole hours standing in front of this pair of apartment blocks on Hipólito Yrigoyen at 2,500, and almost arrived late to the final exam of History II as a result – "Colombo's work is a wonderful monstrosity that goes beyond questions of style." Tano was a fanatic, a defender to the death of the Milanese architect, something that hadn't met with approval during their time at the faculty; in fact, some junior lecturer said in front of Barletta that Colombo's façades were not architecture but decorative fondant, to which Tano yelled from the back of the theatre:

"Stucco, not fondant! Stucco, not fondant!"

And he paid for this spirited defence; they failed him twice on the exam.

"Colombo did what he wanted," insisted Tano. "He didn't give a shit about other people's opinions – that's why the smart families wouldn't employ him, Pablo. Look where his buildings are: Almagro, Balvanera, Boedo; not even one in Barrio Parque or Recoleta."

Pablo Simó hasn't chosen any buildings for Leonor in Barrio Parque or Recoleta, either. Consulting his watch, he sees that there are still ten minutes to go. He wonders whether or not to put *AN* beside the building on Avenida Paraguay at 1,300, chosen because he suspects it will prove to be Leonor's favourite. Technically, Pablo thinks the design may belong to the Liberty Milanese movement, and even though he knows that Liberty Milanese was Italy's art nouveau, he thinks this building deserves its own designation. So he writes down *AN*, and in brackets *LM*. Pablo Simó begins to see that all roads seem to be leading back to the same place in the previous century, although he isn't sure to which movement the balconies on Arenales and Riobamba belong and he can't remember the name of that building's architect. He's always been proud of his love of rationalism; why, given this unique opportunity to show a woman his favourite architecture, has he plumped for art nouveau?

"It's the extravagance of the style, the curves, the exuberance. That's what makes art nouveau sexy, Simó," Tano would surely reply if he were to walk into this bar where Pablo sits drinking a soda that's short on fizz, on this near-deserted avenue.

And even though his friend isn't there and Pablo has no idea where Tano might be now, he imagines him sitting in the opposite chair at the table.

"Since when are you art nouveau, Pablo?" Barletta asks him. "I was the art nouveau one. You were the rationalist, the elegant art deco, and I was the flabby one, even though we both hailed from the same middle class. What's happened to you?"

"Nothing, Tano."

"Nothing? How many years have gone by since we last saw each other? Fifteen? Twenty? Something must have happened to you in all those years, Pablo."

"It's got nothing to do with the passing years, Tano."

"So what is it?"

"It's to do with today – with these last few days."

"Tell me."

"I swear if there were anything by Gaudí in Buenos Aires I'd go and live there right now."

"Gaudí isn't going too far?"

"The more undulations and curves the better."

"You've fallen in love, Pablo!"

"What are you on about?"

"You've fallen in love. I don't think it's a curvaceous building you want to get into, but a curvaceous girl."

"You're mad, Tano. I'm still with Laura."

"And?"

"I'm still married."

"And?"

"So the situation's the same as when we last saw each other."

"Hardly the same – a lot of time has passed, brother. We're older, Pablo. Do you know that I don't know a single guy of our age, I swear, not one, who isn't sick of his wife?"

"Sick?"

"Yes, sick, that is the word Pablo, sick; even if they don't put it that way, you can tell from the way they talk about them – or don't."

"Yes, I am older."

"And more scared, too."

"Scared of what?" Pablo asks.

"That life will always be like this," he answers. "Nothing more than a petty annoyance we have no choice but to endure, a mild annoyance, but permanent all the same, not painful, not fatal, but sapping."

Pablo plays with the napkin dispenser, pressing on the spring until a pile of napkins falls out at once, then he dedicates himself obsessively to replacing them. Without looking at Barletta, his eyes fixed on the action of his hands, he says:

"The girl's just over twenty-five, Tano."

"I told you there was a girl!" Barletta cries, beaming. "Didn't I tell you? Art nouveau my arse!"

"Yes, there is one, and she's pretty and she laughs and she's nice to me," he says, and lets his gaze drift to a bus passing on the avenue outside.

"You're in love, Pablo."

"Do you think? I don't know if this is being in love, Tano. I don't think I know what being in love is. Is it this? Have I finally succumbed?"

But when he shifts his gaze back from the window, Tano Barletta is no longer sitting opposite him. Pablo's on his own now. Alone – and in love? – with his scribbled list of buildings, less preoccupied now by the subject of art nouveau than by whether he, at this stage in his life, can say that he knows what love is. Against what parameter or measure can he check whether what he felt in the past was love or not? It's possible to know what a car is, or a mountain, a bear, an apple, or a plastic napkin dispenser. A corpse buried in the foundations of a building. But what is love, Pablo Simó asks himself today, perhaps for the first time in his life. Is it what he felt for Laura when they first met? Or what he felt later, when they decided to get married? Is love that pain he felt in his chest in the hospital, the day that Francisca was born? Or is love that alteration that Marta Horvat has so often triggered in his body? Is it the reason he is still married? Or is that simply a derivation of love, as Liberty Milanese derived from art nouveau? Is it love that led him to lie to his wife about the reason he wasn't going to the supermarket as he has on so many other Saturdays, or to buy a yellow cardigan and new jeans and sit in this bar waiting for the time of his rendezvous to arrive?

Pablo gazes blankly out of the window. Two girls of Francisca's age pass the window, laughing, and behind them a man alone, and behind him a woman walking a dog. He wonders if any of them know what love is. Does the waiter know, or the cashier? Does Laura? And Marta Horvat? He reckons that even if they do not know, they must believe they do, because love is a democratic concept: everybody claims to recognize it and know or have known about it. For some it's a source of joy, for others woe, but nobody claims ignorance. Even his invented Tano Barletta thinks he has the right to ask him about it, as though he were privy to some higher knowledge. The same Tano Barletta who, as far as Pablo knows, never had a relationship lasting longer than two weeks, who liked to maintain that marriage was for cowards or dullards, whose appreciation of the female sex was limited to a chart he used to carry around in his student days, based on a points system that rated different parts of the candidates' bodies, but principally their bums, thighs and tits. That same Tano Barletta, albeit imaginary, has just assured him that he, Pablo Simó, is in love. Is this another of those chalk/cheese situations? He and Tano Barletta may mean different things by love. The more he looks for answers, the more questions he comes up with. Or perhaps it is simply the same question taking different forms. Because if you aren't sure what love is, what questions are left to be asked? He doesn't know, but Pablo is sure of one thing: that nobody, married, single, male, female, young or old, dares to doubt – as he does today – that love exists.

He looks at his watch – shit, it's five minutes after the time he arranged to meet Leonor. He leaves money for his drink on the table and rushes out, anxious that the girl may already be waiting for him.

Or worse: that she may already have gone, which would go to show precisely how little Pablo Simó knows about love.

12

There are too many people on the corner of Rivadavia and
Callao for a normal Saturday afternoon. And there's too
much noise. Why did he tell her to come here? Only he
would think of asking a woman to meet him in a square
where there are always people protesting with banners, flags,
loudhailers and horns. He tries to see whether she is standing at one of the other corners, straining to see between
the flags; there's no sign of her. Could she be behind that
tall man with the denim jacket? No, that's not her. And it's
not the girl with black shades who's crossing over from the
square; it looks like her but Leonor is shorter, prettier, and
her hair, even when it is tied in a ponytail, shines more. He
turns again, pausing at each of the four possible directions.
Lots of people, but not her, not Leonor. What should he
do now? Just wait? Pablo toys with the zipper on his new
cardigan, pulling it up and down a few inches, as if that
movement makes up for his lack of action. He could call
her to establish whether she has been and gone, or never
came. He takes from his wallet the number that Leonor
wrote down for him on a paper napkin. For the first time
in his life he wishes that he had a mobile phone; today
he feels that he needs one – if he had one she could have
called him, then he would know what to do next and he

wouldn't feel so lost. He casts around him in search of a telephone booth then asks at a news stand, where they tell him that there is a call centre with phones half a block away. He checks his watch: fifteen minutes since the time they agreed to meet – more than fifteen, eighteen, nearly twenty. At the call centre, he dials Leonor's number.

"Are you still coming?" Pablo Simó asks the girl.

"I'm standing on the corner. Where are you?"

He doesn't answer but hangs up, leaves two pesos – more than enough to cover the call – and runs towards the corner of Rivadavia and Callao. From a little way off he sees her. She's wearing a pink jacket – what could that mean? She still has the mobile in her hand, open, as though she were waiting for it to ring again. He runs as fast as he can.

"Hello," Pablo says, trying to disguise his breathlessness, and while he's wondering what to do next, she puts her hand on his shoulder, brings her face close to his and kisses his cheek.

"Hello," she says. "Where were you?"

"In a call centre. I thought you weren't coming."

"I got here a while ago, and as I didn't see you I went to buy some water," Leonor says, indicating the bottle, from which she takes a sip before offering it to him:

"Do you want some?"

He looks at the girl's hand on the bottle but says nothing, and Leonor, interpreting his silence as a "no", takes another drink.

"So where do we start?"

"We're going up Rivadavia first," he tells her.

"What do you mean, 'up' it?"

"In the direction that the numbers get bigger," Pablo answers, and points out the route they need to take.

"Let's go up, then," she says, smiling with her eyes.

They walk along Rivadavia in silence and, although it isn't an uncomfortable silence – quite the opposite – Pablo wonders whether he ought to start a conversation. Why is it always obligatory to talk when you're with someone? Why do most people find it so hard to tolerate silence? He would be happy to continue like this, walking quietly beside her, but he's worried that that the girl will think him nervous or shy, or lacking in things to say. Better for him to do what everyone else would and say something, he decides. He could kick off with the buildings they are going to see and what he knows about them – it would be a good way to show off in front of the girl, but perhaps it's boring to launch into this so early into their walk. The thing is, he doesn't know if he's at liberty to talk to Leonor about anything else. She asked for building façades to photograph and for him to accompany her; that much is clear, but how much else can they talk about as they walk? There's the photography course that Leonor's taking. Or how long it took her to get to their meeting point. There's the brand of mineral water she's carrying and whether she prefers waters with or without sodium. There's the weather. Definitely the weather – who doesn't talk about that? But as soon as he pictures himself saying "Nice day, isn't it?" to this girl, he feels like an idiot. He could ask her who she lives with, if she has a partner, or has had one. No – not unless she asks him first, he decides, and he hopes that Leonor does not ask him, because he would be obliged either to tell her about Laura and Francisca or to lie to her. He looks at her again and decides that waiting for the girl to speak first isn't such a bad option. But they keep walking and Leonor says nothing, though she doesn't seem to find the silence awkward: every so often she looks at him, smiles and drinks water but says nothing. Pablo pauses to let her take a step forward then moves sideways, trying to

117

change their relative positions so that Leonor isn't walking on the outside of the pavement; she doesn't understand the gallantry and looks puzzled by his manoeuvre.

"What's wrong?" the girl asks.

"Nothing," he says, but he tries to make the movement again, touching her lightly on the back to indicate that she should step sideways.

The girl laughs, moves her rucksack as though that were the obstacle to Pablo's positioning, and lets him swap sides.

"What's wrong?" she insists.

"Nothing, just that that's your side and this is mine."

"Why?"

"Because women walk beside the buildings and men beside the street," Pablo explains.

"Really? Who said?"

"I don't know who said it. It's a custom."

"Are you someone who's very attached to customs?"

Pablo feels uneasy; he's not sure what to say. Is he very attached to customs? If so, which ones? After eleven thousand and seventy days with Laura, how can he be sure if the customs he respects are his, hers, or the ones they both agree on? What told him to ask this girl to walk on the inside of the pavement? Leonor, tired of waiting for Pablo to answer her last question, tries another:

"But why – is it because it brings bad luck? Is it like walking under a ladder or crossing the path of a black cat?"

"Something like that," he lies.

"You're very funny," Leonor says, and her eyes stretch into a smile that takes over her whole face.

"Really?" Pablo asks. "I think that's the first time in my life anyone has told me I'm funny."

"Perhaps you're only funny with me," she says, and Pablo feels a tightening within his body. "Do you think?"

"Yes, perhaps," he says.

They wait on a corner for the lights to change; Pablo can see himself reflected in a shop window on the other side of the road. It takes him a moment to recognize himself wearing these uncustomary colours, but he knows the image must be his because beside it is the girl in the pink jacket. When the lights change, he puts his hand on Leonor's waist and guides her past the few people coming the other way and the odd car trying to push through. As soon as they are safely on the other side, he lets her go.

"Is it much further?" she asks.

"Two blocks," he says.

And those two blocks pass without Pablo being able to think too clearly. Since they started walking, the sum of things he knows seems to have been dwindling: he knows that there is a girl in a pink jacket walking beside him, that this woman smells of a light perfume, perhaps not a perfume as such but the scent of a cream or the soap she used to wash herself that morning; that every so often this woman brushes against him as they walk; that he knows her because she came to the studio to ask about Nelson Jara, and that he likes her. He knows, too, that he is walking up Rivadavia following the ascending numbers, that soon the sun will hide itself definitively behind the buildings on his left; he knows that he has a list of art nouveau façades in his pocket along with his wallet and that, even though he hasn't brought the measuring tape, the Caran d'Ache pencil or the notebook, their absence no longer worries him. Leonor takes his arm and leans in to say something to him he doesn't quite catch, because he's wondering if the hand Leonor placed on his arm and has yet to remove may have more significance than as a means of support bringing her closer to his ear to tell him whatever it is she has just told him.

When they reach block 1,900 on Rivadavia, he stops to show her Palanti's building on the other side of the road.

"Which one is it?" she asks.

"That one," he says, pointing at it.

A bus stops in front of them, blocking their view for a few seconds while passengers get on and off. They cross the road and Leonor studies the building for a moment before getting the camera out of her bag to take photographs.

"That's quite a weight they're carrying on their shoulders," Leonor says, pointing to two muscular figures, distant relations of Atlas, who represent men kneeling on cement blocks and appear to bear on their backs the central portion of the building.

"They're not holding it up," he corrects her. "The building has an iron skeleton; those two men are simply decoration."

"Seriously? How do you know?"

"I've seen the plans."

"But they think they're carrying it. Look at their faces."

Pablo looks again at the sculptures and sees that what the girl says is true: those two unburdened men are labouring under a misapprehension, the effort of carrying such a load showing not only in their faces but in the muscles of their arms and backs. Leonor pauses to take a few close-ups of the decorative cherubs on either side of the doorway. Meanwhile Pablo wonders who could have authorized the placement of an air conditioning unit on the front, but only on the right, thus upsetting the harmony of the façade, like someone taking a knife to a cake and cutting it anyhow, with no respect for the natural order of things. Now Leonor walks back across the road to get perspective and take a photograph of the whole frontage. Pablo watches her from his side: her face obscured by the camera, her arms raised to the correct level; her legs slightly separate, feet firmly planted as she tilts for the best angle, as though her body were itself the tripod that would give the portrait its stability. A young man passes, sizing her up in a way Pablo doesn't like. He walks on a few steps, then turns back to look at her again; Leonor doesn't notice, but Pablo's ready to charge across the street, grab the man and say, "What are you looking at, idiot?" He'll never know whether he would have done so, because by the time he gets a chance to cross, the man has gone on his way and Leonor, who has taken all the photos she needs, sees him approaching; oblivious to the reaction she has prompted in two men, she says:

"Which way now?"

"The only way is up," he says, and she laughs.

Pablo helps her put the camera away in her rucksack and arrange it on her shoulder. He offers to carry it for her but she says that isn't necessary: she's used to carrying things.

"Like those guys," says Leonor with a wink, pointing at the stone Atlases they are leaving behind them.

On the way to the next stop, just a block ahead, Pablo Simó thinks of several questions he would like to ask Leonor, but dismisses them one by one: some seem too silly and others too bold. He wants to tell her something she would find interesting, something that reflects well on him, but can't think what. Now could be the time to show off his professional expertise, his knowledge of the city's architecture or of urban planning – but he rejects this gambit as too likely to fail. Could urban planning really be of interest to Leonor? What, he wonders, could such a young woman find to admire in a man of forty-five? Because that is what he would like: for her to admire him.

"You mean you want to seduce her," says Barletta, who has suddenly appeared, this time without Pablo summoning him.

121

"I didn't say 'seduce', I said 'admire'," he says.

"Call things by their names, Pablo."

He tries to make Barletta disappear, concentrating on Leonor and asking:

"Don't you need information about the architects, the technical details and so on?"

"No, I don't think so. I thought I would just put the address under each photo," she says. But a few steps later, the girl changes her mind. "You know what? On second thoughts, a few facts and figures would be good. But another day, when I can sit down and make notes with more time. Would that be OK?"

"Yes, fine," he says.

Pablo Simó walks the rest of that block in silence, thinking only of two of the words uttered just now by Leonor: "another day". If she said it, that's because she thinks they are going to meet again, that there will be another day, another walk, another moment.

"Here it is," he says when they are just about to walk right past it, and he points to the building by Ortega, though without mentioning his name because, for the moment, she's not interested in the architect responsible, though perhaps she will be on "another day".

"Let's cross," says Leonor. "I can't see it properly from so close."

So they cross the road, but the girl, instead of walking onto the pavement, leans against a parked car, as though she were in a cinema seat, and looks up. Meanwhile he looks at her: from this distance she doesn't seem like a girl to him but a woman, and he begins to suspect that Leonor may be older than he thought she was. So why not ask her? Leonor's hip, splayed against the car, attracts him strongly. He crosses over to her. The girl sees him coming, and when he is a few steps away she pats the car's bonnet, three or four times, inviting him to sit next to her. The car is dirty and he knows that Laura would warn him to be mindful of the dust, but he doesn't hesitate for an instant and sits where Leonor tells him.

"Do you know what it's called?" Pablo asks.

"What?"

"The House of the Lilies."

"Why?"

"You see those stems winding their way around the windows up to the roof?" he says, drawing closer as he traces the lilies' path in the air. "Do you see?"

"Yes," says Leonor and she looks hard at the building, her face so close to his that Pablo feels himself on the point of kissing her when she without realizing – or does she? – moves away, slipping her rucksack off her shoulder so as to get out her camera and take more photographs.

While Leonor gets her shots, Pablo studies this building he has chosen for her. The top floor is crowned with the head of a man, or possibly the god Aeolus, presiding over a cornice of lily branches – more meaty and robust that anything you would find in a Buenos Aires garden – some of which are tangled in his hair. The stems begin at the base of the building and run up it, and every so often there is a flower, but the branches have no ends, they rampage over the building, right to its top. They've colonized the man's head, he thinks. If Pablo Simó hadn't studied this building at university, if he didn't know that it was called The House of the Lilies, he would say that this building had fallen into the clutches of man-eating plants.

"Ready," Leonor says, putting her camera back into the rucksack. "Shall we carry on?"

It's more than ten blocks to the next building, which is also on Rivadavia, and Pablo, though not used to long walks, doesn't feel tired. "Stubborn Blood" has been spray-painted onto one of the metal shutters and below it "MP 20 Project for the People". Pablo fixes on the graffiti while Leonor takes her photographs. He wonders whether "Stubborn Blood" is the name of a rock group, one of those Colombian dance bands, some urban tribe, or simply represents a howl of desperation in the midst of a city where so many – he, Leonor, Francisca – live in silence. Or fill the silence with banalities. But never shout, never explode. He suspects that Leonor would understand the reference, but he's not going to ask her; he fears that would serve to highlight the distance between them. The girl takes lots of photographs of the birds adorning the front of the building, then declares herself ready to carry on. How much older is he than this girl? Or should he say woman? Twenty years older? Fifteen? He doesn't know. Quite a bit.

"How old are you?" he asks abruptly as they set off for Colombo's other buildings, this time on Calle Hipólito Yrigoyen.

"Twenty-eight. Why?"

"Curiosity. No other reason."

"Stubborn Blood", thinks Pablo Simó, and does the arithmetic: seventeen years. Up to what age might one continue to have stubborn blood? At what age will Pablo Simó cease to feel this tension in his legs which every so often climbs through his pelvis into the base of his stomach while he walks next to a girl seventeen years younger than him? How much is left – not of life, but of this feeling he has today?

"Art nouveau was ephemeral, Simó," Tano Barletta whispers in his ear. "You know it yourself: no other style ever dated so fast."

124

And even though Tano Barletta isn't there, Pablo knows that what he says is true.

"And you know why? Because people who didn't understand it saw it as exaggerated and sloppy, Pablo, and they even had the nerve to call it 'spaghetti style' like that idiot in History II, do you remember?"

Pablo remembers the reference to "spaghetti style" and how he had had to restrain his friend to stop him thumping the assistant lecturer, and he laughs. Leonor says:

"What's funny?"

"Nothing, just something I remembered," he says.

"Tell me," the girl insists.

"A friend who loved art nouveau and Colombo," Pablo says, and explains, before she asks him, "Colombo is the architect who designed that building I just showed you, with the peacocks on it."

"Were they peacocks?" she asks.

"Yes – what did you think they were?"

"I've no idea, but don't peacocks have long feathers that open out like a fan?"

"The males do," he says, "when they want to seduce a female."

"Those ones didn't want to seduce anyone."

"Perhaps they were female," reasons Pablo.

"But what were you laughing about before?" she asks.

"I don't know; I don't remember," he says, and they both laugh again.

After she has photographed the two buildings by Colombo at Hipólito Yrigoyen 2,500, and he has explained to Leonor what collective housing is, stealing as many glances at her as he can without her noticing, Pablo suggests taking a taxi to the next façade.

"Do you want to take one?"

"Well, aren't you tired?" he asks her.

"No," she says, "but that's fine. If it's far away; perhaps we'd better, to conserve energy."

Conserve energy. Why does Leonor say that? Does she mean she wants to conserve energy for him? Does she want him to conserve energy for her? No, she didn't intend that subtext, he decides, and hails a taxi that has just turned onto the road from Saavedra. Pablo opens the door for her to get in first, then gets in himself; it seems that he really is a man devoted to customs. Once the car is moving, Pablo Simó looks out of the window and takes a moment to clear his mind. The light is beginning to fade and there are things he must resign himself to accepting. For example: that if the taxi driver doesn't hurry, it will be almost dark by the time they reach their last destination; that he is forty-five years old and his companion is twenty-eight; that by now Laura will be putting away the supermarket shop and waiting in vain to go to the cinema; that he wants to seduce this girl and he still doesn't know how – yes, Barletta, *seduce*; that the car they are travelling in has just stopped at a red light and that means the loss of another moment of daylight. But in spite of everything – the lack of sun, his age, his wife, the failing light, the supermarket and cinema, the traffic – sitting there, just inches from Leonor, he feels happy.

The taxi stops on Riobamba and Arenales, as instructed by Pablo; he pays and they get out. Leonor tries out different corners to find the best angle from which to photograph the balconies: black ironwork railings covered in flowers that are open like perfect Spanish fans or like Manila shawls. Out of curiosity, while she's taking the photographs, he walks around the corner looking for the granite block where the architect's signature should be engraved. He wonders if anyone, if any of the few pedestrians walking past them on this Saturday evening cares who made this building, who thought of it, imagined it, who drew it on paper like Pablo Simó draws his eleven-storey north-facing tower; who, in contrast to him, put it up. First he finds the name of the building: Camerou, and then on another stone block, the name of the architect: P. Pater. The same one who designed the Tigre Hotel, he thinks, and instinctively he looks for Leonor, to share his discovery, then thinks better of it: she said that she didn't want that sort of detail now; "another day" she said, and he wants her to admire him, to see how much he knows, to see that he can teach her all kinds of things – but he also wants that other day to exist.

From there they carry on up Paraguay to 1,300 and to the building that Pablo chose specially for Leonor, standing as it does for Liberty and for femininity. It surprises him, annoys him in fact, to see that a dry-cleaner has taken over the ground floor. He can't remember what used to be in that space, if he ever knew, and, even though it's closed for the day, there is someone working inside and Pablo Simó feels that the smell of warm fabric and dry-cleaning chemicals don't go with this building. Until recently, the majority of buildings in Buenos Aires were designed to accommodate commercial premises on the ground floor, so the look of the building at street level was determined by luck, misfortune or the highest bidder. Often an art deco building, or one that's rationalist, art nouveau or some other style, ends up in the care of greengrocers, electricians, hairdressers, bars and betting shops; the *coups de grâce* are the boxes of merchandise going in and rubbish bags coming out, the parade of customers, the curtains that open or close depending on the time of day. Pablo definitely doesn't like the presence of a dry-cleaners here; the steam emitted by the machines every so often makes the building feel clammy and heavy, oppressive in a way that doesn't chime with that clear, almost white façade on which a sequence of tiles evokes a striking but peaceful image of the country.

"I'd rather any kind of business on the ground floor than the utter lack of respect for pedestrians with which buildings are put up in this city today, Pablo." It's Tano Barletta again. "Nobody cares any more about pedestrian identity. Walk past these great towers set back from the road and you could be in any part of the world. São Paulo, Miami, Madrid – it's all the same."

Although Pablo Simó definitely doesn't like the dry-cleaners stuck in there, he also does not want, in the middle of his walk with Leonor, to get into an argument with Tano Barletta, especially not about architecture. He wants to be alone with her, strolling through the city, seeking out interesting places, holding her rucksack while she takes photos, touching her – accidentally? – as they walk, looking at her. Tano Barletta, right now, is out of place. Could he have a conversation with Leonor about the city's lack of respect for pedestrians? He doesn't think so, but it doesn't matter. He hasn't talked much to Laura either about architectural matters during all their years of marriage, or if he has it was only under the heading of "work", as another man might talk to his wife about his day at the office, in a bank or in an operating theatre. He has talked about architecture with Marta:

"Have you noticed that new buildings in Buenos Aires today are made to be looked at from a passing car?" he said to Marta one day when they were in a taxi negotiating the slopes of Belgrano, on their way to the showroom that had just opened in one of the most recent projects by Borla and Associates.

"So?" she asked.

"It's a shame. Buenos Aires used not to be like that. Buenos Aires was a place for walking."

"It is a place for walking if you don't have a car. You don't have a car, right?"

But this isn't the day to be thinking of Marta, either.

"Do you like it?" Pablo asks Leonor quickly, to get Barletta, Laura and Marta Horvat out of his head.

Leonor doesn't seem to hear him. She's moving her lens over the façade covered with tiles brought specially from Milan and the high, narrow balconies with their ornate white railings, looking for her next shot.

"Do you like it?" he asks her again.

"It's a bit naive, isn't it?" she says and surprises him, not only with the observation, but by suddenly turning the camera on him.

"Why me?" says Pablo, covering his face.

She laughs, takes another picture of him and says:

"Because."

Leonor moves in front of Pablo, experimenting with different angles while he plays at hiding, at putting on silly faces, sticking out his tongue, and finally he grabs the camera and takes a picture of her, and then another, and another until Leonor is posing for him as naturally as Pablo sketches a building.

"You seriously think it's naive?" says Pablo, and when he gives back the camera he lets his hand cover Leonor's for a moment, without caring whether the girl realizes it's not accidental.

"Yes, I seriously do. I don't know – isn't it a bit silly? If I had to choose between this guy with a bull or the other one with lilies in his hair, I think I'd choose the other one."

"But they're not men," he says. "They're sculptures and mosaics."

"The thing is that I don't know anything about sculptures and mosaics," she says, looking at him intently.

Stupid, stupid man, Pablo tells himself, before Barletta says it for him, and while the girl takes her last photographs he turns his attention to the picture formed by the tiles: a peasant woman and a man herding an animal, one on each side of the balcony. A few of the original tiles are missing and he wonders how they came to be replaced by plain ones that wilfully disrupt the composition. Leonor seems not to have noticed this. He knows that Tano Barletta would also have detected these hiccups in the imagery and that it would bother him equally – but Tano Barletta is barred for what little remains of this city walk. It would have been better not to fill the gaps revealed by the missing tiles, he thinks, to show that there was a loss it wasn't possible to make good, rather than deceive the onlooker by covering them with any old thing.

"That's it," says Leonor. She puts the camera away with a decisiveness that makes it clear there will be no more photographs that day; then, without prevarication, with a spontaneity he has come to expect of her, she adds:

"Do you want to come back to my place for a bit?"

Pablo freezes for a moment, wondering if he heard correctly but, looking at her, he sees that she is waiting for an answer. Yes, he heard right.

"The two of us?" he asks her, immediately berating himself for saying something so stupid, a man of his age to a girl seventeen years his junior.

"If you want to, yes: I'm inviting you," Leonor says.

And he wants to, of course he wants to, it's what he wants more than anything.

13

Following custom – whose custom? – Leonor gets into the taxi first and for that reason, when she directs the driver to Giribone and Virrey Loreto, Pablo Simó, who's settling into his seat and about to close the door, hears only "Loreto". That name, being all he hears, isn't enough for him to make an association between the place where they're going and the studio where he works. The sun has set now, but the streetlights are not yet on, and that penumbra between the dying afternoon and the coming night makes him feel strangely giddy. He's sitting very close to her, too close – he hears her breathing, hears her laughter and watches her unpainted lips; and beneath the lips the teeth, white, young. And still looking at them, Pablo remembers that she has invited him to her house without specifying what the invitation is for. She didn't say it was "to have a coffee", "to eat something", not even "for a chat" or to "watch a film", and that lack of certainty gives him vertigo. He remembers her words clearly, because she said them only a few minutes ago: "Do you want to come back to my place for a bit?" Just like that.

Pablo glances out of the window then back at her; she has closed her eyes now, as if wanting to rest after a long day. He looks out of the window again; he can't really believe that he's going with this girl to her house, can't imagine what will happen once they get there, and as if in need of confirmation that he deserves none of this, he mentally replays the fatal moment in which he asked "the two of us?" – and that makes him feel insecure and foolish.

As they get closer, Pablo picks out certain streets, recognizes places, reads illuminated signs he has read before. However, none of this is sufficiently familiar to ring alarm bells, because for years he has been going to work underground, crossing the city beneath its surface, changing twice in a journey that is shaped like a narrow horseshoe and re-emerging only when he reaches the corner nearest to his studio. Nobody understands why he chooses this route, which is longer than the journey he would make by bus, but Pablo Simó likes it. So what he sees now, although it prompts in him that feeling you get when you meet a person you know from somewhere but can't recall where, doesn't actually surprise him, and Pablo still makes no connection between the view through the window and their destination.

He steals another glance at her. First the face, and as she is still asleep, or at least has her eyes closed, he dares to let his gaze drift downward, past Leonor's neck, her breasts, her waist, her stomach. Her thighs are squeezed into tight jeans and he knows now with a certainty that he would like to undress them, touch them, move his hand up between her legs and leave it right there, touching her for as long as she will let him while he feels the thrum of his own stubborn blood surging up through his legs.

Only as they pass the bar where he and she met for the first time outside the studio does Pablo fully become aware of his surroundings. Even then, despite a slight consternation, he reminds himself that that day, in the bar where he never usually goes, she had said:

"I live near here. I've moved into the area."

The relief doesn't last long. As the taxi drives right past the Borla and Associates studio it slows down and Leonor, as though responding to an interior alarm bell, opens her eyes, looks outside and says:

"Just a few yards further on."

"This all right for you?" asks the taxi driver, coming to a stop in front of the building where Nelson Jara used to live.

"Yes, perfect," she says.

Then the girl waits for Pablo to take out money to pay for the trip, but he doesn't – he's distracted, his mind somewhere else, struggling to fathom whether what has happened is the product of chance or fate. The taxi driver repeats the fare and Leonor, not waiting any longer, opens her rucksack and takes out a few notes, but Pablo reacts just in time:

"No, please, let me," he says, and pays.

They enter the building and walk through the hall towards the lift. She catches sight of herself in the mirror, makes some comment about her hair and laughs; Pablo tells himself that they aren't going to 5C, that they can't be going to 5C, the flat where Nelson Jara lived, the one that he, Pablo Simó, still reproaches himself for never having entered in order to see the crack that man told him so much about – and he tries to focus all his attention on Leonor, on some part of Leonor's body, her perfume or her smell, on what it will be like to touch her, kiss her, caress her, and he promises himself that Jara will not ruin this moment. But when they are inside the lift she pushes the button for the fifth floor, and even though the action causes her to rub against him, exciting him, Pablo feels that once again, he is fighting body-to-body with Jara. The floors stack up underneath them, one by one, until the lift stops at the fifth floor. Pablo opens the door, Leonor steps out; the corridor is dark and the girl fumbles for the light, bumping into Pablo and laughing. He laughs too, not out of amusement but because he is so nervous. The light goes on, she looks at him with a certain provocation (does she look at him with a certain provocation?), she walks ahead of him and, even though Pablo is silently praying that she won't do this, that she won't stop in front of door C and put the key she's playing with at the moment into the lock, Leonor stops there anyway, in front of this door, her back to him while he follows in a daze. He waits behind her while the girl gropes for the lock, puts her key into it, and some difficulty in turning it makes her lean back, scarcely bending from the waist, but it's enough to bring her body even closer to his and she rubs against him again. Then Leonor opens the door and motions him inside. Pablo nods, but gestures for her to go in first, then he follows her inside.

They go in together, very close to one another. She puts on the light and he immediately looks for the crack in the wall. He can't see it – has it been covered perhaps? If so, when? And by whom? He doesn't know. Leonor smiles at him; she puts down the rucksack and he suddenly realizes that the crack may be hidden behind an Indian cloth that is attached to the side wall, like a hanging or a false curtain. Leonor takes off her jacket and he discovers all over again her neck, the hands arranging her hair, her firm breasts which are coming towards him, which are definitely coming his way, which stop in front of him and wait. And Pablo's breathing becomes agitated, his thighs harden and his hands prick; he thinks he has to do something, knows he must do something, and just as he is about to decide what exactly he will do, Leonor kisses him. Simple as that, without asking permission: standing in front of him, looking into his eyes, she lifts her arms to encircle his neck, barely opens her mouth while looking at his, pauses for a second then kisses him. And he lets himself be kissed and kisses her, and holds her, pressing this woman's body against his, running his hands up and down Leonor's back as though looking for something, feeling her breasts against his chest and her pelvis against his pelvis and his thighs between her thighs. He kisses her, his tongue running over her lips and probing her mouth, going in and out – God forbid he should be clumsy – until Leonor finally pulls away from him and, without taking her eyes off his, lies down on the floor and beckons to him, pulling him down to lie on top of her. And when Pablo lies on her and moves his face close to hers to kiss her again, the girl puts her mouth to his ear and says:

"Third place on the list of my favourite things: making love on a wooden floor that smells of wax."

And then he comes undone on her and she on the waxed floor and it seems that Pablo has succeeded in forgetting where he is, has forgotten about the Indian hanging, the wall behind it and Jara himself. But a minute later she twists to the side and climbs on top of him and now Pablo, from his new position, prostrate on the wood floor, can't help but fix on the wall that he knows, once and for all, he will have to see. For some reason, what's hidden by the hanging fuels his excitement, and as he goes inside the girl who's moving back and forth on top of him, as he runs his hands over her, bites her, possesses her, penetrates her, Pablo Simó can't stop thinking about the crack and that, the image of the slashed wall superimposed on the warm and sweaty body rocking on top of him, brings all the tension in his own body to a climax more powerful than anything he remembers experiencing before, and with it relief, as he lies next to her.

After a few moments lying like this in each other's arms, Leonor gets up and goes to the bathroom.

"Back in a minute," she says.

Pablo is left alone on the floor, staring at the wall-hanging, scrutinizing it, following the arabesques in burgundy, ochre and black as though they were hieroglyphs he needed to decipher. He stands up and, still with his eyes on the fabric, puts his trousers back on, pulls up his zipper and, bare-chested, bare-footed, approaches the wall. The material hangs from a rod improvised from a wooden stick and thick braided cords attached to two gold-coloured hooks hammered in at the wall's edges. Pablo thinks that this cloth is masquerading as something it isn't, that it's not a curtain, nor a hanging or a picture, though it pretends to be one of those things. Even though he thinks he knows what it conceals, in spite of that inevitability, as he stands in front of the cloth. Pablo feels strange, uncomfortable and even shaken. He doesn't yet dare to look, and it's as if this wall and he were sizing each other up, as he and Jara once did. So Pablo Simó waits, he's not sure what for – a sign, permission or something finally to make him draw aside this veil and look at last. He takes one step forward, positioning himself within touching distance of the hanging, and does just that – touches it – holding it a few inches away from the wall for an instant, running his fingers over the border but nothing more, as if his three-year wait demanded some sort of ceremony before he dare go further. Because he feels at fault: he knows that he ought to have come here at the time, he should have examined the crack, he should have evaluated its significance and repaired it. But he didn't, Jara himself had told him not to, that there was no need:

all he wanted was the money. Over my dead body, Borla had said. And so he never went.

Leonor calls from the bathroom, "I'll be right with you, OK?"

It's the prospect of her return, of her naked body distracting him from the task in hand, that induces him to lift up the cloth – before he thinks better of it, before he runs out of there like a coward – to see what is underneath. And even though he finds exactly what he was expecting, exactly what he *didn't* want to see three years ago – Jara's wall bisected by a crack as-yet unmended – something in what he sees, as his eyes move along its extent, strikes him as unusual.

"What are you looking at?" she says, standing behind him, wrapped in a short towel that barely covers her groin.

Pablo doesn't answer; he holds the cloth in one hand and runs the other one over the crack, up high, as far as he can reach and then downwards; he assesses its width, which is consistent along its length; he puts his finger into the crack to estimate its depth and verifies this as not greater than half an inch. He pays special attention to the biro marks all the way along it, measuring the distance between them with his thumb and index finger, and he could swear that it is always the same – two inches? And then he is left in no doubt: the width, the length and the depth of that crack are regular and calculated. Somebody must have planned and drawn it, then chipped at the wall until the fissure appeared.

"I'm going to get it fixed when I have some spare cash. It's not serious, is it?" Leonor asks.

Pablo shakes his head and, feeling a mix of rage and admiration for Jara, he smiles and says:

"No, it's not serious."

137

This time he can say it with total certainty. Because now Pablo Simó knows that the crack – which he hadn't wanted to see, which prompted the events leading to Jara's death and everything that followed – wasn't caused by soil movement, or the pit they sank, or the building they put up. Today he knows that the crack was created by Jara himself, painstakingly, inch by inch, across the wall.

And that Jara, the man he buried that night within the foundations of the building where he now works, deceived him. That Nelson Jara – why did he never see this before? – was just as much vermin as is Pablo himself.

14

Over the three years that have passed since the night they buried Jara under the building from which the Borla and Associates architectural studio now operates, Pablo has constructed and reconstructed countless versions of the events leading to the entombment, finally arriving at one that seems plausible and may be definitive – though he will never know for sure. He has pieced it together going on what he saw, heard, touched and even smelled that night; on what Marta Horvat and Borla told him; but also on his own conjecture based on sources that, though less reliable, are more instinctive: deduction, suspicions and hunches.

That night began for Pablo a little after three o'clock in the morning. Laura had been asleep for some time and he had fallen into that dozy state that precedes deep sleep when the telephone rang. Waking with a start, he answered quickly; Laura merely turned onto her side, as though a sharp ringing in the middle of the night were bothersome but not worth waking up for. It was Marta Horvat; she seemed to be crying, saying things that Pablo couldn't get straight in his head, and he didn't know if that was because he was still half-asleep, because Marta was incoherent or because of the excitement of getting a call from her at that time of night.

"Speak to Borla," Marta said. "You've got to ring him at home, his mobile is switched off. Tell him to come right now to the Giribone site."

Pablo rubbed his face, groped for the wristwatch he had left on the bedside table he didn't know how long before, looked at the time and said:

"You think I can ring him at home at this time of night?"

"I couldn't, but you can," Marta replied.

"Why can I?"

"Because his wife won't have a fit if it's you calling, Pablo," said Marta bluntly, and then she ordered, "Call him right now."

Pablo knew he ought to say something, but couldn't think what. Beside him, Laura opened her eyes, looked at him, and seemed surprised to see him sitting up in the middle of the night, silently holding the receiver against his ear, but just as Pablo was thinking up some explanation for his wife, she turned away from him and pulled the pillow over her head. Then Marta Horvat repeated her instruction again, this time in a helpless tone Pablo didn't remember having heard before.

"Call him, Pablo, please."

"It's all right, I'll call him, don't worry," he said. "Is there a message I can pass on? Some problem with the work?"

"Tell him that Jara's…ruined everything and that…" she broke off. "Nothing else. Tell him that, and to come quickly."

Pablo remembered Jara, that afternoon, sitting opposite him at the table in Las Violetas, bent on doing whatever it took to stop the cementing going ahead, and he wondered if he had tried to carry out his threat; but he couldn't ask Marta for any details because she was now really crying on the other end of the phone. He would have loved to put his arms around her, hold her face against his shoulder,

140

dry her tears one by one; he would have told her that the fault lay with him, Pablo Simó, and nowhere else, because he hadn't known how to stop the man in time, because he hadn't gone to check on the crack as he should, hoping that the little he had done would be enough. But that now he would do everything to stop him, for her sake and so that she wouldn't cry any more. Pablo Simó would have loved to do that and many other things besides, however Marta Horvat hadn't asked for his help or consolation; she only wanted him to act as an intermediary in making the call to Borla. It hardly even qualified as a minor role.

Pablo got up and looked for his address book; despite having worked with him for so many years, he had only occasionally called Borla at home, and even though he had a good memory for his clients' telephone numbers or those of suppliers or developers, he knew that he would struggle to remember his boss's, given the time of night and the disorientating urgency of Marta's call. He dialled from the kitchen extension, so as not to wake Laura; after three rings, Borla's wife answered, sounding as bewildered as he had been minutes before, when Marta had woken him up.

"Hello Señora, good evening, and forgive my ringing at this time. I'm Pablo Simó and I'm calling because…" he said, and he would have carried on explaining himself, except that he heard the woman at the other end of the line holding the receiver away and saying, "It's for you, Mario."

To start with, when Pablo began telling him about Marta's call, Borla sounded strange and disengaged; Pablo suspected that it was possibly not the first time that she had found some pretext to wake him in the night. But when he finally uttered the name Nelson Jara, Borla seemed to grasp that, at least on this occasion, there was a serious motive for the call.

141

"What a bastard," Borla said, more to himself than to Pablo. "I'll go to the site straight away, thanks," and then he hung up.

So it was done – he had fulfilled his part of the deal. Today he reproaches himself for not leaving it at that, for not sticking to his minor role and going back to bed with his wife after carrying out Marta's instructions. But there was no more chance of sleeping that night and Pablo was beset by a different set of recriminations. He couldn't help berating himself for not having known how to handle Jara. He reproached himself for each of the things he now realized he should have said to Marta before hanging up. He could have reacted better after the shock of the call and taken charge of the situation when he spoke to Borla, by saying something like: Do you want me to go with you? Shall I drop you off at Giribone in case you need some help? Shall I go instead of you? Why trouble yourself in the middle of the night? Let me go – I know Jara and I can handle the situation. But there was the crux that was bound to doom any belated attempts to help solve this intractable problem: he had not yet proved himself able to handle Jara and he knew that at some point, the next morning, the next day, when things were calmer, Marta and Borla were going to throw his failure in his face.

He walked around the house, back and forth between the kitchen and the bedrooms countless times; he went into Francisca's room and looked at his sleeping daughter; he dialled Marta's mobile number but hung up before it rang; he put on the television in the living room and zapped between channels without taking anything in; he dialled Marta's number again and it went to answerphone, but he didn't leave a message; he made himself a coffee and drank it looking out of the steamed-up window, wiping it first with his hand and then with the voile curtain – something Laura would have forbidden, had she seen it – until the whole pane was transparent; he washed the cup; he rang Marta's mobile again and it went straight to messages again; he went back into Francisca's room and then into his own. His daughter and his wife slept on. He got dressed in the same clothes he had taken off the night before, located his Caran d'Ache pencil in the jacket pocket, tore a page out of his smooth-paged notebook and wrote a note for Laura, explaining that there had been a problem at one of the worksites and that he was leaving earlier than usual – as early as four o'clock in the morning, in fact, although he left out the detail of the time.

Down he went to the street and to the entrance of the underground, but the padlocked metal gates reminded him that the last train had gone hours ago and it was still a long time before the first one of the morning. He looked up and down the street: at that time of day Avenida Rivadavia seemed unworldly, deserted and silent. He stopped the first taxi to pass, and once he had sat down realized, too late, that he didn't like it – it was old, untidy, the card bearing the driver's particulars was smudged, its tatty plastic cover sticky and dusty – but he didn't dare get out and wait for another one, so with resignation he said, "Calle Giribone."

When the driver asked him what number, he chose one two blocks before the site where Marta was crying because – so he thought – Jara had managed to stop the base slab being laid the following day. He still wasn't sure what he was going to do, whether he would simply watch from a safe distance or whether he would be bold enough to step forward and offer his help, in spite of his recent run of failures.

Once out of the taxi, he began to walk. The street was badly lit, and so Pablo was barely twenty yards away before he could confirm that the car parked in front of the entrance to the site was Borla's. He stopped beside the security fence, leaning against it in the hope of hearing something that would throw light on what was happening inside, and he waited. Even from this side of the wooden fence he could smell damp earth. In the distance, barely discernible, he thought he could hear Marta's voice, or not so much her voice as a jagged wail, like an anguished hiccuping that every so often rose above another clearer and more defined sound: that of gushing water. He pushed the gate and found it open; his foot struck some hard object and, bending down to pick it up, he saw that it was the padlock that was used to secure the entrance gates at night. As soon as he started to walk he felt his shoes sinking in the mud. It was too dark to see anybody, but as he moved forward the noise of running water got louder and the sound of Marta crying seemed to disappear – or had he imagined it when he thought he heard it before? He stepped into a deep puddle and felt the force of the liquid pushing his foot away, how the bubbles crowded the water's surface then burst beside his shoe, under his shoe, in front of his shoe. To one side of the puddle a spade was stuck in the ground, like the flag of a victorious climber arriving at the summit of a mountain; somebody – Jara, who else? – had used it to dig down to the mains water supply and ruptured the pipe. Once again, he remembered that meeting with Jara the previous afternoon at Las Violetas, when he had said:

"If it has to rain, it will rain, Simó."

The water was bursting out like a spring, spreading over the ground and draining into the pit. Looking up, Pablo tried to pick out Jara's window; there was no light in it, but he waited and watched, half-expecting the man to appear at any moment from behind his curtain. Could it be that Jara, after flooding the plot, had gone home and was watching now, relishing the consequences of his action? Jara was definitely capable of that, Pablo thought, and of much else besides – but he would soon find out that he was mistaken.

He walked on and out of the middle of the puddle. First he found Marta, kneeling beside a column, her clothes covered in mud and her muddy hands clawing at her face, not caring about the state she was in, shaking her head from one side to the other as if to say no, that this wasn't real, that this couldn't be happening. And Borla was standing a yard away, staring vacantly into the pit. A single bulb hanging inside the workshop partially lit up the area; Pablo was surprised to see the workshop open; the door seemed to have been forced and the nightwatchman was nowhere to be seen. Indecipherable sounds came from a badly tuned radio inside, and on top of a table and benches improvised from bricks were the remains of a dinner for two: a pizza box with some portions still in it, two pieces of card that must have served as plates, two plastic glasses and two bottles of red wine: one empty, one opened but almost full. Pablo walked towards Marta and stood beside her, waiting for her reaction; when he saw that she was neither surprised nor angered by his presence, he said:

"Don't worry, Marta. We can repair the pipes at first light and if the weather's on our side we can still pour the cement tomorrow, in spite of Jara."

She lifted her head and looked straight into his eyes. Now she did seem angry, but not with him – was she angry about Jara's act of destruction? In fact she looked devastated, as if this were not the footprint of a building under construction but the site of a battle she had lost. For a moment she stared at him, watching him with desperation, halfway between screaming and subsiding again into tears. And then, in an effort to speak, for all that her teeth were chattering and she was trembling from shock, rather than cold, she said:

"Go and take a look inside the pit."

Pablo was scared then; he saw that what Marta had just said contained a meaning he couldn't yet decipher, that when she said, "Take a look inside in the pit," she wasn't merely sending him to look at more mud and water. He walked towards where Borla was standing, almost at the lip of the open ground.

"Hello," Pablo said.

"Ah, Pablo." Borla didn't seem surprised to see him. "It's a good thing you came. I won't be able to do this alone," he said, and he nodded towards a point inside the pit, not far from where they were standing.

Pablo tried to accustom his eyes to the lack of light, and when he was able to focus he understood what was happening: six yards below them a body hung on its back, like a cloth draped over a table, held up by the reinforcement bars in the shuttering of one of the open footings in the pit that was waiting to be filled with cement.

"Jara?" he asked, though he already knew the answer.

"Yes, Jara," Borla said.

"What happened?"

"He slipped…He was arguing with Marta. He went mad, completely lost it, and he slipped."

Hearing her own name was a trigger for Marta to start crying again, more wretchedly than ever. Pablo turned round to look at her; she was clutching her head, her whole body shaking uncontrollably.

"Have you called an ambulance?" he asked.

146

"He's dead, Pablo," Borla said. "Do you think calling an ambulance would be helpful?"

"What about the police?" he insisted.

Borla turned to look at him then spoke slowly, enunciating the words as though he had already decided on them before Pablo's arrival:

"I don't know. I was just about to call them when you arrived, but then I started wondering if it was for the best. What do you think?" he asked, but didn't wait for Pablo's answer. "Do you know how long they'll close the site because of an accident like this? A month at least, maybe two months. We can forget about meeting deadlines, about our commitments and especially our salaries. You know very well that if we don't have work under way on the building it will be much harder to sell. I don't even want to think about this, but if word gets out that somebody died here, the superstitious just won't want to buy. There are so many buildings in Buenos Aires – why choose one where a man got killed? And if we can't sell quickly, Pablo, you know what will happen: our flow of income is cut off. We've got too much in play at the moment. There's no cushion."

Borla fell silent for a moment, ostensibly leaving Pablo a chance to digest what he had just said, though more likely with the intention of letting him appropriate it, this idea that was not his. Then, when he judged that the necessary time had passed, he posed the question again, as though Pablo's opinion really mattered to him.

"What shall we do? What do you think?"

And when Pablo still seemed unsure, Borla continued:

"My main concern is her." He nodded towards Marta Horvat. "They're going to arrest her, however much we explain that the guy was a bastard, that he tried to blackmail us, that he planned this fiasco to extort money out of us. You know what he did? He made friends with the nightwatch-man, he turned up with a radio so that they could listen to the Argentina v. Brazil match. He brought a pizza, wine, and when the guy wasn't paying attention he locked him in the workshop. Thank God the nightwatchman had his mobile on him and called Marta, and she called you and you me. Well, you already know that part. By the time Marta arrived, Jara had already broken the mains pipe with a spade and caused this quagmire. I tried to shut off the mains supply from the street, but I couldn't – I didn't have the right tools. First thing tomorrow we'll have to send a team in."

Borla took a minute to survey the damage around him and give Pablo a chance to do the same. Then he said:

"Marta says he seemed like a man possessed, that when she arrived Jara was holding up the spade like a trophy and laughing like a child, or like a madman. I can just imagine him, can't you?"

Pablo nodded. Borla went on:

"He asked her for money. You know how much he asked for? Thirty thousand dollars! Talk about a brass neck! Had he mentioned such a high figure to you?"

"He told me he was after money, but he didn't specify how much."

"Well, tonight he certainly did specify it, spelt it out. Now tell me, Pablo, do you think we should have to swallow such a bitter pill, when everything, absolutely everything, is his fault?"

"I don't know," said Pablo. "All the same, I think the police —"

"The police what? You really think the police are required here?" asked Borla, and went on: "And to top it all, he tried to touch her. That dirty old pervert tried to touch Marta."

"Jara?"

"Yes, Jara."

Pablo could picture Jara jumping around with his spade after breaking a water pipe, but he had difficulty picturing the same man trying to touch Marta. He had never given the slightest indication of being interested in Marta or finding her attractive; he had never even made the kind of jokes that Pablo often heard other men make about women as devastatingly pretty as her. Jara seemed more anodyne, the kind of man who may once have known what it was like to be with a woman but for whom sex had long since ceased to be a priority. His only priority as far as Pablo could see had been to lay his hands on the money he thought they owed him for the crack that had appeared in his wall – had he really asked for thirty thousand dollars? – and there was no need to touch Marta Horvat for that. Pablo turned to look at her again: she was crying like a little girl now, hugging her knees, and, without letting her legs go, cracking the fingers of one hand with the other. Could it be true? He found it hard to believe, but if it was, if Jara had really groped Marta or tried it on, Pablo Simó would personally kill him – if he weren't already dead.

Borla said, dropping his voice – Pablo guessed with the aim of protecting Marta:

"He touched her and was taking her off somewhere, so she tried to shake him off and that's when the guy slipped and fell into the pit. I can't help thinking, and I don't think anyone would judge me for it – that it was really a piece of luck this man fell in before he had a chance to do something to Marta that neither you nor I would have forgiven."

Neither you nor I. Pablo was surprised by the certainty with which Borla counted him among the defenders of Marta's virtue, but it was true, all the same: he would never have forgiven it. He examined the pit's muddy walls for marks left by Jara's body as it fell: skids or grooves made by his feet as he slipped; he wanted to imagine the fall, the thud, the death. The light was bad and water was still sweeping over everything; he guessed that that was why he couldn't see any marks at all.

"I ask you, again, what use will the police be? We know that this was an accident, befalling a first-class shit, a would-be rapist. But that doesn't alter anything: not the time during which the work will be stopped, nor people's superstitions, nor the police, nor the problems that this may end up bringing her. You go and explain all that to the cops and spend however many days you get inside until they can prove that you're not lying, that it was an accident or, as a last resort, that it was self-defence. Can you see Marta in prison?"

And Pablo couldn't see her there, nor did he want to. Borla lit a cigarette, then asked him:

"Has this guy got any family?"

"I don't think so. He told me once that he lived alone…" Pablo didn't elucidate further, but he did remember the calculations Jara had made that same afternoon to show how much each of them was spending on electricity.

"That's good, Pablo. It's better for him not to have relations. It gives us a freer hand."

"You're thinking…"

"Yes, I'm thinking that, given the circumstances, the best thing is for Jara to disappear without trace. To choose the other path – to face up to the situation and tell the truth – would still leave this man in the same place, but not us, at least not without paying a very high price first. It won't be too difficult to put him in the middle of the footing, don't you think? And then tomorrow afternoon, when this mud finally dries, we'll tip cement over the bastard and bury him

once and for all. Not a conventional burial, but in short…
What do you say?"

"I don't know," Pablo replied.

"You can't not know, Pablo, there's no alternative. The man's dead. It was an accident, there's no family – nobody's going to go looking for him under the concrete. You and I have to take this decision. We're the ones who ended up being here; what choice do we have? You can't walk away from every eventuality unscathed – sometimes life puts you in places where you have to decide which side you're on. Which side are you on, Pablo?"

And Pablo decided, that night, that he was on Marta's side – for what other side could he be on? If Marta Horvat needed him, he was going to stand beside her, so he said:

"All right then, let's put him in the footing."

"Well done Pablo, it's the right decision. There are no witnesses other than us three to what's going to happen, so in that respect we can rest easy."

"And the nightwatchman?"

"He doesn't know anything, at least not about the accident. We opened the door to the workshop after Jara had already fallen in, and what with the shock he could scarcely even get into the taxi I ordered him; anyway, he's conscious that to a certain extent this is his fault – at least, I don't know if it is, but I was careful to spell out his part in what happened: he was the one who opened the door to Jara, allowing him to create this mayhem; he accepted the pizza; he compromised site security in order to listen to some lousy qualifier; he drank on the job. When he was in the taxi I got him to wind down the window, and you know what I said to him? I said, 'You're lucky that Jara went away without hurting anyone, but tomorrow we're going to have a conversation about who's shouldering the cost of all this damage.' Listen, Pablo, I've been in this profession a long time, and if there's one thing I know about people like that – believe me, he won't be coming back."

Pablo had already given his agreement, but he still wasn't completely convinced about what he was going to do in a few minutes' time. Then, as if she had intuited his doubts, Marta got up and walked with difficulty the short distance between them. When she was very close to him she said, "Can I count on you, Pablo?"

Anxiously she waited for his answer, standing in the middle of what looked like a pigsty. Tears mixed with mud had made a mess of her face, but Marta Horvat was as beautiful as ever to Pablo, perhaps even more beautiful, as if the night's travails had taken the hard edge off some of her features.

"Yes, of course you can count on me," he said, and so sealed the pact that would bind him for life.

Then he went into the workshop to look for a ladder, trying not to notice the half-eaten portions of cold pizza or the glasses with dregs of wine. But he stopped by Jara's radio, picked it up and held it for a minute before turning it off. When he came out again with the ladder, Borla was squatting beside Marta, stroking her hair. Pablo waited, with his back turned, until Borla left her and came to join him and finish what they had decided to do. Between them they positioned the ladder without reference to Jara's body, but choosing the corner of the pit furthest from the leaking water, where the ground was firmest. Borla went down first, and then Pablo, but together they covered the few steps to where Jara's body hung in the footing, and before either one dared to touch the body they stood looking at it for a while in silence, as if this final act of contemplation were part of the burial ceremony. Finally Pablo said:

"Are you sure that he's dead?"

"Yes," said Borla, categorically, not to leave room for doubt. "Grab him by the feet."

"What if he's just unconscious?" Pablo insisted.

Borla, looking annoyed, stopped to think for a moment and seemed to be about to say something before finally reaching over to get hold of one of Jara's arms. He took his pulse while looking straight into Pablo's eyes and said:

"Dead."

Then, without letting go of that arm, he seized the other, stood up and ordered, "Let's get this over and done with." Then Borla pulled Jara's arms, manoeuvring the body towards him so that he could take hold of it under the arms. And he repeated, "Come on, grab his feet."

The first glimmers of daylight were beginning to appear behind neighbouring buildings; a glow illuminated them, the same that would in a few minutes filter through Jara's window. Pablo made himself look at this man's face for the last time; he had a birthmark on his forehead, his eyes were open very wide and his mouth formed an expression that seemed to have been cut off in mid-articulation, as if Nelson Jara had been speaking when he died. Borla dragged the body over to where he could drop him in the centre of the footing.

"Bring him over this side," he said to Pablo, "and then let go of him."

But, although Pablo moved the body over as Borla requested, he couldn't let go of him. An oblique ray of light falling across the dead man's face now showed more clearly what Pablo had first thought to be a superficial mark: Jara had taken a blow to the forehead. He could see a wound and something dark that looked like blood.

"Let him go," Borla said again, but Pablo was transfixed by what he had seen. "What's going on, man?"

"His forehead," Pablo murmured, and he had the impression Borla knew what he was talking about.

"Just let him go, Pablo, get on with it. Let him go, I said."

In the face of his inaction, Borla dropped the body. Pablo's hands were locked onto Jara's ankles, but they couldn't contend with a dead weight, and even though Pablo Simó wanted to hold onto him, even though he tried – at least that is what he believes and honours in his final version of that night – the muddy body slipped out of his grasp as he felt himself losing a hold on the dirty skin, the old nylon socks and ugly pleated shoes that he knew so well, until Jara finally fell into the bottom of the footing, almost without a sound, sliding down its sides, leaving no trace except for the mud on Pablo's dirty hands, those hands that still throbbed from their recent futile effort.

"Done," said Borla with relief.

"His forehead," Pablo said again.

Borla paid no heed; he was already on his way back up the ladder. Pablo Simó waited a few more moments beside the improvised tomb, then followed him. Once at the top, he saw how Borla embraced Marta Horvat, who was no longer crying but was still trembling.

"It's all right, Marta, don't be upset. It's over," Borla said, consoling her, and as he held her he said to Pablo, "It would be good to tidy things up a bit. I don't know – throw some earth in over him, put the ladder back where it was, clean up the leftovers in the workshop, don't you think?"

Pablo went to get the spade, climbed back into the pit and shovelled earth into the footing. It was the work of a few movements, but he made them with enormous energy, almost with violence, gripping the spade's wooden handle so hard it hurt his knuckles. Then he retraced his steps, climbing up the ladder and pulling it out after him. For a moment he stood on the edge looking into the pit, which was now completely lit up by the early-morning sun. Patiently he kept looking, even though there was nothing to see there now but mud, footings, formwork and their own footsteps, gradually dissolving in the mud and water.

"We'd better go and wash, then come back before everyone else arrives," Borla said. "Pablo, as soon as you can get back here I want you stationed beside the footing. Nobody but you is allowed within two yards of it until everything has dried and the cement's gone in. And you, Marta, stay at home this morning…"

"No, I want to be here," she said.

"Rest first," Borla insisted. "We'll take care of everything, I promise. Why don't you come in the afternoon? This isn't going to dry before lunch anyway and I don't want people to see that you're upset."

Marta said nothing, but seemed to understand. Each one of them had their orders. Borla would drive her home in the car; she would let herself be driven. Pablo would take responsibility for making the pizza, the wine and Jara's radio disappear.

"But be quick about it, Pablo, because I'm going to have to give you a lift home. No taxi will pick you up looking like that."

Before heading for Borla's car, Marta came over to Pablo and said, "Thank you."

He looked into her eyes as they filled with tears again, and at the wet T-shirt clinging to her body, the nipples, the breasts that rose as she sighed deeply and at Borla's muddy hand, invariably present on Marta's shoulder. She cracked her knuckles again and said:

155

"I mean it – thank you so much."

Pablo smiled as much as he was able: it was an effort to say anything lucid in the context of his own exhaustion, Marta's grief and the strange sensation of not knowing for sure whether he had just taken part in a crime or an act of heroism.

"It's fine, don't worry. We did what we had to do," he said finally to this woman whom he had so often desired and whom, at that moment, on that night, he desired more than ever.

But no sooner had she disappeared behind the security fence than Pablo began to question what he had just said. *We did what we had to do?* And from that night until the present day he had continued to question the rationale without finding a satisfactory answer. Then, as now, the deed was done: he had agreed to it, he had brought the ladder and gone into the pit with Borla, he had lifted Nelson Jara by his feet in order to let him slide down into the footing. And as if that were not enough, he had been the one charged with restoring normality while Marta and Borla waited for him in the car, perhaps in each other's arms, perhaps kissing each other.

The remains of the supper went into the skip: pizza, glasses, the empty bottle and the full one, Jara's radio. No, not the radio. He took two steps away from the skip, then went back for it with the idea of hurling it into the footing from the edge of the pit, so that Jara had something of his own to take with him. He stuck his hand deep into the skip's debris and rummaged through the remains of pizza and the wine bottles until he felt an object he took to be Jara's radio. Pulling it out, though, he found that it wasn't a radio but a hammer; Pablo Simó was about to chuck it back in the skip when he felt something sticky and knew instinctively that it wasn't mud. He looked at the hammer and then at his dirty fingers, then back at the hammer; there was no doubt that it was blood.

Pablo walked a few steps away from the skip, squatted down by the broken pipe, washed the hammer until there were no traces of blood, dried it with his own T-shirt and only then, when there were no remaining marks, did he put it back in the workshop from where it should never have been taken that night.

And he left.

15

"What's going on? What are you doing here?"

This is what Pablo Simó says, turning away from the cracked wall to face Leonor.

"Who are you?" he demands.

"What?" she says.

Without answering, Pablo watches her for a moment then, with sudden determination, walks over to Leonor's rucksack, opens it and delves inside as though he knows very well what he is looking for. The camera slips in his hands and nearly falls to the floor, but Pablo manages to retrieve it and return it to the rucksack.

"What are you doing?" she says angrily.

Leonor wrests the rucksack away from him, takes out the camera and checks that it's not damaged, but Pablo keeps hold of her wallet and moves away from the girl as he looks through it. She goes after him.

"Are you mad? Can you tell me what's going on?"

Pablo finds banknotes, a telephone card, a strip of small pills – contraceptives? – and receipts. He ignores everything but the identity card. Leonor makes a lunge for her wallet; he grabs her wrist and says:

"Who are you? You're the daughter, aren't you?"

"Whose daughter?"

"Jara's daughter."

Leonor says nothing and he shouts:

"Are you the daughter or not?"

"No, I'm not Jara's daughter. And give me back my things," Leonor demands, but Pablo ignores her. He brings the ID card close to his eyes and reads:

"Leonor Corell," he says and looks back at her. "Who are you, then?"

"You hardly need me to tell you since you're holding my ID in your hand."

"Why do you live in this apartment?"

"Because it's mine."

"Did you inherit it?"

"Something like that."

"What were you to Jara?"

"Nothing you need to know about."

"A niece?"

"No."

"What, then? His lover?"

"Don't be ridiculous."

"Just tell me."

"Why should I?"

Pablo waits deliberately, watching her, and then says:

"Because I lied to you…"

"You lied to me about what?"

"When I said I didn't know anything about Nelson Jara. I do know, I've always known, and of course I also knew the day that you came asking after him."

"So what, exactly, do you know?"

He draws out another pause and she gets annoyed.

"Just tell me what you know."

"I know where he is."

"Where is he?"

"First tell me why you're living here."

"Is he coming back?"

"No, I suppose not."

"Does he know that I live here?"

"No."

"Are you going to tell him?"

"No, if you and I can come to a proper agreement," says Pablo, and now he does return the wallet and identity card.

"And what would constitute a proper agreement between you and me?"

"One that benefits both of us."

"Such as…?"

"For my part, I want you to answer the questions I've already put to you: who you are, why you're living in this apartment and why you came to the studio to ask after Jara."

"And what will be the benefit for me?"

"That I promise not to tell Jara or anyone else that you're living here."

"Did he go abroad?"

"That doesn't matter."

"Why didn't he keep up payments on the bills?"

"I suppose he thought that it would end up costing him more than he could recoup. This flat isn't worth much."

"He could have rented it."

"He could, yes. If he knew that you'd moved in he could even charge you a bit of rent."

"Are you going to tell him?"

"No, I've just proposed a deal."

Leonor looks at him and rearranges the towel, which has been dislodged by the confrontation, exposing one of her nipples. For a moment they stand watching each other in silence. And the proximity induces Pablo to stop thinking of Jara and think instead that by simply reaching out and pulling away the towel he could be caressing Leonor's naked body again, touching her breasts and feeling her nipples harden under his hand, moving down to her belly, following the line down between her legs to linger there and finally lose himself in her, forgetting about Jara and reclaiming that person he was just a moment ago, perhaps for the first and only time. But he looks in her eyes and sees that Leonor isn't thinking along the same lines at all; she's thinking that Nelson Jara could take away her home.

"Why should I trust you?"

"Because you haven't got many alternatives. I know that you're in a flat that isn't yours, and that's already more information than you'd like me to have. The rest doesn't really change anything – the why, the how – it's all anecdotal. Think of it as a whim: I just want to know what happened."

She watches him, as though sizing him up. Then she says:

"OK, you're right. Even with what you already know you could totally screw things up for me."

"I could, yes…"

"So the deal is still on?"

"It's still on."

"Right," she says, and she bends down to gather up the banknotes, the strip of pills and the telephone card.

Pablo watches her: Leonor squatting, holding her towel around her, each one of the vertebrae on her curving spine defined, a sizable mole under her bottom rib. He imagines the two points that mark the start of her coccyx hidden under the towel. The girl finishes arranging the things in her wallet and stands up, still holding in her hand the receipts, which she looks at briefly then balls up and throws onto the table. Pablo follows her movements with the same desire he felt just now when they were making love on the wooden floor that smells of wax. She seems to realize and says:

"Do you mind if I get dressed before we carry on?"

"No, of course not, you go and get dressed."

"I won't be long," she says, and leaves the room.

Pablo is left alone. He glances at the things around him, feeling guiltily that, whatever Leonor's reasons for being here, he has misrepresented himself in front of her. He wonders if this table belonged to Jara, if these are the chairs he once sat on, if the watercolour hanging next to the front door would also have been his, or if Leonor brought it when she came to live here. Then he returns to the crack. He stands in front of it, lifts the cloth, studies the gash in the wall and touches it again, running his finger along it, and in doing so he can't help smiling with the same sense of wry defeat he would feel if a friend had just taken the last point off him with two fours and a horse in a game of *truco*. Pablo, with all his cards on the table and the game already lost, knows that the crack never existed, that what Jara photographed and what he has in front of him now was deliberately carved into the wall, inch by inch. He knows finally, three years after the fact, that Nelson was vermin, the same as him. And the realization makes him smile. But, even after that revelation, the burden he has felt since the night he let Jara's dead body fall into a footing to be entombed in concrete isn't about to disappear. Pablo Simó feels not relief but the opposite, because his discovery, rather than mitigating his actions at the time, makes him believe – rightly or wrongly – that Nelson Jara and he were not so different from one another. And he can't help imagining himself entering this apartment three

162

years ago, when Jara was still alive, to do what he ought to have done there and then: personally evaluate the crack.

If he had done that – if he had come to the flat and seen it for himself – on realizing that the crack wasn't the product of soil movement but of a man's handiwork, of the very man standing behind him waiting for a verdict, Pablo Simó would have spun on his heel, looked him in the eye and said, "You're a scumbag, Jara." But he wouldn't have got angry, he would have laughed, and Nelson Jara, who would initially have denied everything, would have had to give in when presented with the evidence, and above all in the face of Pablo's laughter, and he would have laughed too, they would have had a beer together and they would have worked out how he, Pablo Simó, having decided this time to put himself on the side to which he belonged, was going to help a fellow scumbag to get what he wanted.

Leonor returns with a bottle of soft drink and two glasses. She's wearing – as always – jeans and a white T-shirt, but she's still barefoot like him. Pablo picks up his own T-shirt and puts it on, too, while she lays the things she has brought out on the table, then sits down and offers him a drink.

"Want some?"

"OK," he says, and he sits down too, opposite her. As he does so, Pablo's bare foot grazes Leonor's and he notices how she swiftly withdraws it at his touch. He grieves to think he may have thrown everything away. And immediately he wonders what that "everything" might have amounted to. Was it really necessary to look behind the cloth that very day? Was it necessary to pressure Leonor into talking? Was it necessary to behave with a violence he didn't recognize in himself, going through her things, rebuking her? Pablo tells himself that, although perhaps none of these things was necessary, they were inevitable, and he suspects – he is almost certain of the fact – that he is going to leave this house with some answers, but without Leonor.

They drink, watching each other over the rims of their glasses.

"Am I going to regret confiding in you?" she asks him.

"I don't think so."

"Look, if you betray me, I'll be merciless."

"I'm not going to betray you," he says, and he tries to imagine what "merciless" might signify for this girl.

Leonor looks at him while taking another sip of lemonade and then, just when she seems ready to start talking, she unexpectedly gets up, goes back to her room without explanation and returns with an enormous bar of dark chocolate. She opens it, carefully to start with, but when the foil won't peel away easily she tears it off, breaks off a piece and offers it to him.

"Do you want some?"

"No thanks," he says. "Number one on your list of favourite things?"

"Number one, yes."

Leonor plays with the chocolate without yet eating it, making it spin on the tray, stopping it suddenly then spinning it again, repeating the action several times before she finally says:

"I've been working with a lawyer for four years, nearly five; I started working with him not long after I arrived here from Mar del Plata. Dr Delpech, the guy's called. He works in debt collection. Someone owes money, someone else wants to call in the debt and can't – Delpech takes on the case, chases the debtor, puts pressure on him, whatever it takes to scare the debtor and make him pay up. I handle the admin – the papers, the procedures. We work with people who are behind with their rent, or with the monthly payments on their appliances or someone with a loan of a couple of grand that they took out to get a new car and then couldn't pay off. Two-bit jobs, nothing, small change."

She cuts the bar in half, offers him one of the pieces again, and again Pablo declines it. She eats it. He waits, but when Leonor has finished she doesn't immediately return to her theme but plays again with the paper, as if she were ordering the words in her head before speaking them aloud. Or summoning up courage.

"Carry on," Pablo says.

"OK, well that's Delpech's business. Or his front, because his real business is something else."

The girl drinks the rest of the lemonade and looks at him. Then she takes Pablo's glass and drinks the little he had left, too. She wraps up the chocolate like someone trying to convince herself she won't eat more. Pablo is tempted to take her hands, to stop their constant activity and hold them, stroke them, but before he has a chance Leonor abandons the chocolate and now one of her hands fiddles with her hair while the fingers of the other drum a repetitive rhythm on the tabletop. He doesn't take her hands; he knows that he shouldn't. It would come too late now, a gesture out of time and place, something to which he no longer has the right. Barletta himself, standing behind Leonor, says:

"Man, what a dickhead. You really screwed that up. Was Jara's crack that important to you?"

Leonor looks at him, her hands lying calmly on the table now. Pablo is relieved to note that her anger seems almost entirely gone.

"I'm going to ask some questions too," she says, and Barletta disappears. "After I fulfil my part of the deal, will you give me answers to what I want to know?"

He nods; he knows he's made a deal, but it worries him to think what of interest he may have to offer this girl.

"You don't want to know what Delpech's real business is?"

"Yes, of course."

"You still can't guess?"

"No."

"Taking over other people's flats."

"What?"

"Identifying properties to usurp."

"Usurp?"

"That's what the lawyers call it: usurpation. According to Delpech it's the legal term for it. There are cases cropping up almost every day: a man, or a family or whoever gets into a house that may have owners but isn't inhabited, and as time goes by not even a judge can get them out. Squatters – you know what I'm talking about, right?"

"Was Jara working for you, then?"

"No, no. Delpech has a network of informers in the administrations of residents' associations, in some rental agencies, among caretakers. When someone finds out that a worthwhile apartment is accumulating significant debt and that the owner is nowhere to be seen, he goes with a locksmith, gains entry, changes the locks and starts paying the bills – the electricity, gas, whatever. And after a while, if all goes to plan, if the owner doesn't turn up and there are no heirs, he starts to rent it out. The idea is that, a few years later, after a period of time stipulated in law, Delpech will put his name to these properties and make money out of them."

"If they don't put him in prison first."

"He's not breaking any law. He doesn't take anything away from the owners or legitimate heirs. Delpech always says that if he didn't take over those flats they'd go to the state, to the same coffers where everything they take from us ends up."

"You mean he's some kind of Robin Hood, your lawyer?"

"No, come on, I'm not that naive. I know that he's not whiter than white. But who is? Look around you, the people that you know. Did they get everything fair and square? That architect you work for, the investors who fund his projects, your neighbours, the guy you're selling your next apartment to – was all their money made above board? And what about the people we see on TV? Or the politicians? Even you, yourself: have you never in your life done something a bit shady? Why should other people get away with it and not us? Those are the rules of the game – and we weren't the ones who invented them."

Pablo doesn't answer, and he wonders if he will ever be brave enough to tell her – supposing their relationship doesn't end badly and for good tonight when he leaves the apartment – that he, Pablo Simó, buried Jara beneath the concrete of the building next door. He keeps asking himself the question, but has no answer for either her or himself. Then Leonor continues:

"Everybody's played the system, Simó, you know that – some more than others, but they've still done it. And if they haven't done it, they're going to one day, and if they don't end up doing it, they're going to regret it; nobody wants to be the chump."

"So how did you play it?"

"I kept this flat for myself. When it first turned up I started by doing the work I always do for Delpech: asking for title deeds, checking whether there were heirs, doing a search on any long-term debt, to see if there were any moratoria we could exploit. The apartment was clean, and I don't know what came over me or exactly when I made the decision, but I remember that I was on my way to Delpech's office, holding my report, making a mental calculation of what it would be necessary to put down to secure the flat, and just as I was about to open the door and go into his office this question popped into my mind: 'And why not for me?' That's exactly what I thought: 'Why not for me?' And right there I turned round and went back to my desk. I put the folder in a box and bided my time. I hadn't mentioned to Delpech that I was working on this flat; by this stage I hardly ever consulted him, I just went to him with the final package. I told him how much a place was worth, how much he would need to pay, and then he made a decision. Even so, I was cautious, in case he came by the information some other way. I waited a month, two months, and after nearly three months I decided to start paying off the debts myself. I let another two months go by and still nothing had happened. So then I went with a locksmith. The caretaker didn't bat an eyelid because he had given me the information himself and been paid for it, but I still didn't move in."

"When was that?"

"About two years ago."

"So why have you only just moved in?"

"Because I've recently split up with someone. I used to live with my boyfriend, who had moved here from Mar del Plata first. When I came, he had a little flat that belonged to his grandmother that nobody was living in. So I didn't need a place because we were living together. This flat was more like an investment, to have something of my own. Everybody needs something, right? But anyway, events conspired. I had to move out very quickly, and that was how I wound up here."

If Leonor believes Pablo Simó to be absorbed in the story

of how she ended up with Nelson Jara's apartment, she's wrong. Pablo is thinking about that boyfriend she used to live with. And he wonders if the girl still loves him, or if he loves her, why she hasn't mentioned him before, why they split up and if the split is definitive. Pablo Simó would like to ask Leonor Corell these questions, but he knows that none of them is permissible under the terms of their pact.

"What are you thinking?" she asks him.

"Nothing."

"You think I'm a monster."

"No, of course not. Everyone plays the system – you said so yourself."

"So what have you done, Simó?"

"Is that what you wanted to ask me?"

"It's one of the questions I have."

"I haven't done anything," he lies.

"Well, then it's about time you started."

"It's about time, yes."

Pablo Simó wishes he could turn back time, return to the moment they were lying together on the wooden floor and kiss her again, and get on top of Leonor, caress her, enter her.

"I have something to show you, something I'm sure you'll be interested in," she says then.

"What?"

"When I moved in I did a thorough clean – the place was disgusting, nobody had cleaned it for years. There was even a cup with some remains in it, milk I suppose, that was full of maggots and giving off a stench I can still smell sometimes. Can you smell it?"

"No."

"I can, I suppose just because it made an impression on me," she says and, as if the smell really were still there, she sniffs her hands. "I cleaned everything on my own. I didn't ask anyone to help me, so as not to arouse suspicion. My hands were raw from so much scrubbing. After that, after the deep clean, I wanted to throw away all the junk Jara had kept everywhere. That was when I found these boxes under his bed, and inside one of them was all this information about his building and about Borla's studio that I couldn't really understand: Jara's last diary was there with appointments, calculations, photos. I don't know, there was so much stuff mentioning Borla and Associates that you would think there was nothing in this man's life that mattered more to him. So I thought it would be better to go and meet you and find out if you knew anything about him. You remember when I went to see you?"

"Yes, I remember." Of course he remembers.

"I had the rucksack stuffed with Jara's papers – I don't know why, just in case. I thought perhaps you might need them. Shall I show you your book?"

"What book?"

"There's a book that has your name on the cover and your photo."

Pablo is stunned. Leonor goes to her room again and a minute later reappears with a box she puts on the table and then opens. Pablo instantly recognizes Jara's plastic bags and his orange folders; the very same ones the man thrust at him in their first meeting, the ones he had with him when he stood at the door to the studio waiting in vain that day that Pablo spied on him from the opposite corner then fled like a coward. But Leonor, rifling through the box, takes out something he has not seen before: an exercise book with his name written in a cursive hand and a photograph of him, blown up in a colour photocopy.

"Do you want to read it? Have a look."

And Pablo doesn't know if he wants to, but he takes the book and flicks through it without daring to focus on the personal information in front of him. He feels as if he were holding his own diary – but written by someone else. And he doesn't want Leonor to witness his reaction to the book when he does read it.

"Do you mind if I take this away? I'd like to have a proper look at it. Anyway, it's getting late and I ought to go – it's been a very long day."

"Long and strange," she says, and smiles in that distinctive way that makes Pablo forget about the world. "Take it, yes. But after you read it you're going to have to tell me if everything he says in it is true. That's what I wanted to ask you; that's my part of the deal."

"Have you read it?"

"Yes, pretty much."

"And?"

"Well – it's all about you," says Leonor, and she smiles again.

Pablo gathers up his things, puts on his yellow cardigan and his shoes.

"Right, I'm going."

He moves towards the door. Leonor goes with him, turns the key and opens the door. He looks at her and makes as though to kiss her on the cheek, but the girl takes his chin, and turns his face just enough that his mouth faces hers, then presses her lips against his in a brief, gentle kiss. It's more than Pablo feels he deserves. Why did she move her bare foot away when he brushed against it, if she's kissing him on the lips now?

"Women are like that," Barletta tells him.

He waits for a moment, but he knows that he can't expect more of Leonor this evening. So he steps away from her, walks towards the lift, pushes the button and waits. She waits too, in the doorway, until the lift arrives, and then they wave to one another, without saying anything else. Pablo opens the lift door, goes in and closes it, and as he presses the ground-floor button he hears the sound of the door to Leonor's apartment closing.

The lift jerks into action, removing Pablo Simó from view and with him the book written by Nelson Jara.

16

On the underground, Pablo Simó sits with the book on his knees. He looks at the cover, tracing with one finger the letters, written by hand in thick, black ink, that spell out his name. Then he turns his attention to the photo, which must be more than ten years old, and wonders where Jara could have found it. He suspects that it's the photograph from his student identity card at the School of Architecture; he's sure that there's no other photograph of him wearing that shirt with the thick purple lines – though Laura insists they're blue – which never wholly convinced him but which he certainly wore that day. He remembers it well because his wife had given it to him for a wedding anniversary that happened to coincide with the day identity cards were renewed in the architecture department, and Laura had insisted on him wearing it – even to the point of making him take off the shirt he already had on to change it for this purple striped one. How did Jara get a copy of that photograph? Pablo doesn't know. Nor does he know what's stopping him from opening the notebook. He tells himself that he would rather take his time over it at home. Looking at his watch, he sees that it is nearly eleven o'clock at night; it's going to be difficult to explain his lateness to Laura. But he doesn't feel worried, and much less sorry;

it was worth running the risk for all kinds of reasons: he got to walk through the city with a girl he thinks he's in love with. He kissed her, caressed her, and, in a wonderful encounter far surpassing any fantasy he might have had before their meeting, he made love to her. Besides (and it shames him to put this other revelation on a par with making love to Leonor) he established that Jara's crack was nothing more than a fraud fabricated by the man himself. That alone may be justification enough for braving Laura's anger. He closes his eyes and, letting himself be rocked by the motion of the carriage as it lurches from one station to the next, he imagines Jara marking up the wall according to the sketch that he wants his fake crack to follow, standing on a chair, using a plastic ruler to measure the distance between each twist of the fissure he is going to carve, joining up the points – would he use a cross, a dot or a dash to make each mark? – and then drawing in every stroke of the crack exactly as he had imagined it, chipping at the wall above the drawing with a chisel, a gouge, even a screwdriver. And once the groove was opened, he imagines the man brushing out the debris, blowing on the crack to dislodge dust and plaster, shaking off any fragments of the wall still clinging to his clothes and finally sweeping up the rubble with obsessive care just as he, Pablo Simó, would have done in his place.

The train comes into a station, slows and stops. Pablo opens his eyes and looks for the name: Callao. There are two more stops before he has to get out and change lines. He looks again at the notebook, *his* book; in a way it makes him feel important – if Jara dedicated one entirely to him, he must have deserved it. Or did he also write one for Borla and another for Marta Horvat? He resolves to ask Leonor the next time he sees her, or when they next talk, and to ask her for these other books, if they exist. The next time he sees her, he thinks, as the train sets off again. He closes his eyes, imagining Leonor naked. He wonders if there'll be another chance to see her like that and promises himself that there will be and that this time Jara won't be allowed to spoil things, especially not now that he knows that everything to do with that man and the crack was a fraud, an invention. Well, not absolutely everything: his corpse, or what's left of it, is still buried under the cement, that's for sure. That, regardless of any lies Jara may have told, remains true. It will always be true.

He changes trains first at Carlos Pellegrini and then at Avenida de Mayo, where he finally gets onto the line that will take him home. He dozes, but wakes up just in time to get out at his stop, Castro Barros. Outside he's dazed by the lights of a Saturday night in Buenos Aires. The cars don't hurtle past the way they would on a weekday and there are groups of young people out on the street. A man walks past him – surely on his way to a date – fresh from the shower and smelling strongly of aftershave. As Pablo continues towards his house, he hears laughter, murmurs, a car horn, another horn answering it, screeching brakes, another horn, somebody shouting to a friend from the other side of the avenue, a rowing couple making up with a kiss. The smell of pizza gusts over him and Pablo realizes that he's hungry – how many hours is it since he last ate? A boy wearing a sweatshirt with the logo of a local pizzeria passes him carrying a pile of takeaway boxes, confirming that his senses don't lie.

He's yards away now from the building where he lives and he wonders if he ought to be fabricating some sort of excuse to explain his lateness to Laura: the usual work complications; Borla's lack of consideration when he's not the one in a hurry; the reduced frequency of underground trains on weekends. In spite of his trepidation, Pablo Simó dares to hope that Laura will still be in a good mood, as she has been these last few days, and that his lateness won't have given her a reason to be annoyed or irritable as she usually is. He prays that she went to the cinema without him, that she enjoyed the film and is flung in an armchair now, glass of wine in hand, or in bed watching another film on TV, maybe even an old one she's seen several times, while she waits for him. He wonders if his wife will suspect that he's been making love to someone else. He smells his hands, checking that they don't smell of Leonor, and even though it's necessary to conceal from Laura what he was doing only a few hours earlier, it saddens Pablo Simó not to have the girl's smell still on his body. He pulls up the collar of his cardigan to sniff that too, and although he picks up a scent that isn't his and isn't recognizable, he takes it to be a new clothes smell – the starch or fabric softener the garment was washed in before it was put on sale – whatever, but definitely not Leonor's smell.

However, Pablo's hopes are simply that: hopes, and as soon as he puts his key in the door, before he's even opened it, he can hear Laura crying. It's tempting to pull the key out again and run away, but that's not an option – he wouldn't be capable of it. So he does what he ought to do: he opens the door and goes in. On the other side of it is Laura, her face a picture of devastation, the blue vein pulsing above her left eye, clutching a handkerchief which every so often she dabs her eyes with, blows her nose on or bites as if it were guilty of some terrible thing that has happened. Pablo struggles to understand what his wife is saying, but even though it surprises him that his late arrival one Saturday after twenty years of marriage should cause such a scandal, it never occurs to him that Laura's wailing might have some other cause than him and his romance – romance? – with Leonor Corell. He tries to make sense of a few broken phrases he can pick out from the midst of howling and hiccupy sobbing, but however much he tries, it all sounds incoherent. Could Laura know more than he suspects? Could she have followed him, spied on him? No, she couldn't, he tells himself – but then why is she shouting, why does she grab onto his jacket, as though he might be about to escape, why does she say, breathlessly, "I want to kill myself," and then release him and throw herself onto the armchair, weeping disconsolately? Pablo doesn't dare ask her what has happened, because he knows that she has already said it, between howls, perhaps even more than once, although he wasn't able to understand, and he also knows that if his wife repeats it in this state, he still won't be able to understand. He waits for Laura to catch her breath, to calm her weeping, to control her hiccups and lower her voice. When she manages that and says again, "I want to kill myself," the words sound clear, modulated in every syllable, without shrieking, and are therefore intelligible to Pablo, who happens to say that it's not that bad, that he was at work, that it got much later than he had realized, but before he has finished Laura's fury grows again and she shouts:

"If this isn't 'that bad', what is 'that bad' for you?"

That much he hears – loud and clear – but he still doesn't grasp the significance. Then Laura complains that if he had been there that afternoon, perhaps the girl wouldn't have stopped being what she is, but at least she, Laura, would not have had to be alone at that awful moment, alone when she slapped her, alone when she kicked her friend out of the house. It's only then that Pablo Simó realizes that when his wife says "the girl" she isn't referring to Leonor, but to Francisca, and he feels greatly relieved, though simultaneously bored of this family drama, which seems to be dragging on indefinitely. Laura's screaming now that this is the worst thing that has ever happened in her life, she screams that even his – Pablo Simó's – death would not be such a grave event, because that is the law of nature and everyone must die some day, a theory Pablo agrees with, although they have never talked about it, but not this, she repeats, not this. Pablo, not understanding what "this" refers to, asks his wife:

"What do you mean by 'this', Laura?"

"Haven't you been listening to me, Pablo?"

"Yes, but try not to shout and to be a little more clear. Otherwise I can't understand you."

"You'd like me to be clear?"

"Yes…"

"Really clear?"

"Yes – of course."

"Your daughter's a dyke, Pablo," says Laura, exaggeratedly opening not only her mouth, but also her eyes and even her nostrils.

"My daughter's a what?" he asks.

"A dyke! Are you going to tell me now that you don't know what a dyke is?"

"Dyke?"

"A lesbian, gay, homosexual…"

"Francisca?"

"Yes, Pablo, Francisca. Have you got any other daughters?"

"Where did you get that from?"

"I went into her room and I found her and her dyke friend, sucking each other's faces off."

"Ana?"

178

"Yes, that revolting —"

"They were kissing?"

"They were halfway down each other's throats, Pablo. Mouths open, tongues inside one another. You can't imagine what it was like for me to see them, the shock I had. Our daughter was never butch. She was a sweet little girl. The other one was, but not her. How could I even have imagined…" And once again Laura swaps shouting for weeping.

Pablo goes to the kitchen and returns with a glass of water for his wife. Francisca appears in the doorway of the corridor that leads to the bedrooms. She looks at him, he looks at her; Laura, with her back to her daughter, is saved a moment's disgust. The girl's face is misshapen, swollen from crying, and her eyes look inflamed and red, more from anger, Pablo suspects, than from grief.

"Can you come to my room a moment, Dad?" says Francisca in a stifled, barely audible voice.

But Laura hears her and before Pablo can say anything, without turning to look at her daughter, she yells:

"Get out of here you disgusting animal, get out!"

And the girl returns to her room, putting up no more resistance than a hateful face.

"Laura, do you think it's helpful to treat her like that?"

"I treat her in the way I'm able, in the way that comes naturally, in the way she deserves."

"What does she say about it?" he asks.

"She's got nothing to say – what would you expect her to say? Does it matter what she says, Pablo?"

"Let me speak to her."

"There's nothing to talk about. What do you want to talk about? What it's like playing tonsil tennis with another woman?"

"Why don't you take a pill to calm yourself down?"

"Because I've already had three and they made absolutely no difference."

"Then have a wine, or a whisky, whatever it takes to unwind a bit. The way you are at the moment isn't going to help solve anything."

"Because this has no solution, Pablo – that's what you seem not to understand. How the hell do you solve the fact that your daughter is a lesbian? Is there a lesbian help centre? Is there a rehab farm, like for drug addicts? Is there some new kind of medication?"

"Let me speak to her."

"Do what you want," says Laura, getting up abruptly and spilling the water left in her glass, then disappearing down the same corridor along which Francisca also disappeared a moment ago, with the same aim of shutting herself in her room behind a slammed door.

Pablo waits a few minutes before going to his daughter's room. He pours himself a glass of water, drinks and thinks about what he is going to say. He doesn't really know. Probably it's better to let Francisca speak first, he thinks; after all, she did ask him to go to her room. Remembering that makes it easier to broach his journey down the corridor; however, when he gets to Francisca's room he still doesn't feel ready to face her and lingers by the door, waiting, he's not sure what for. His daughter is listening to music, but he can hear her sobbing even though the sound's turned up. He waits a moment more, captive to the music, which he likes although he doesn't know it, and the weeping, which pains him, as if the two elements combined to form an improvised duet that sounds better than expected. Finally he takes a couple of deep breaths and knocks on the door, saying:

"It's Daddy, can I come in?"

Francisca doesn't respond, but after a few minutes the handle turns and the door opens just enough to let Pablo know that he has permission to go in. He does so, cautiously, as though asking for approval with every step. The room is illuminated only by the computer screen from which the music emanates. The girl is sitting on the floor, leaning against the wall, hugging her knees. Pablo moves aside some large cushions and sits on the edge of the bed.

"What are you listening to?"

"Leonard Cohen."

"Where did you get it from?"

"It was recorded for me by a friend who's good at finding weird stuff," she says, wiping her nose with the back of her hand. "Do you know him?"

"No," he says. "Should I?"

"If you like it, yes; if not, no. There's no point in listening to someone you don't like."

"I do like this guy."

"I can make you a copy if you like."

"Go on then. Who's the friend that's good at finding weird stuff?"

"Toni."

"Do I know him?"

"He's the guy I sometimes meet up with after school, the one Mum doesn't like because he has a beard."

"Today your mother must be wishing she'd never said a word against Toni and his beard," he says with a smile, which she returns. "Toni knows his music."

"Do you lot ever listen to music?" Francisca asks.

"Us lot?"

"You and Mum."

Pablo hesitates, not answering, as though Francisca's question posed some difficulty in answering. She says:

"I mean, I've never seen either of you listening to music at home. Do you listen to music somewhere else, like at the office?"

"Yes, sometimes I listen to it at the office," he lies.

"I'm going to play you my favourite song," says Francisca.

And while she goes to the computer to select the track she wants to share with him, Pablo wonders why he hardly listens to music when, up until a few years ago – fifteen? twenty? – it occupied an important place in his life. He wasn't ever an expert or a passionate fan, but he enjoyed it. And Tano Barletta too; they used to listen to all kinds of things during the long nights they stayed awake working on presentations for the faculty. Barletta really did know about music: everything he made Pablo listen to was good, unusual – like what Toni finds for Francisca – a "jewel", Tano used to say. Even without his passionate endorsements, Pablo had to admit that Barletta's choice in music reached him, got right inside him and moved him. Tano is bound to know of Leonard Cohen, Pablo thinks, and his gaze falls once more on his daughter, sitting against the wall and hugging her legs. Even the scant light falling on her face is sufficient confirmation of her beauty, her youth and her desolation. Why is his daughter, at this early stage in her life, as desolate as he is? Can that kind of misery be genetic or inherited, he wonders? Are some of us predisposed to be crushed by events that pass by others leaving no mark? Why do some suffer what others barely notice? Cohen's music isn't helping. It only seems to underscore his own sense of desolation.

"Did she tell you?" Francisca asks.

"Mum? Yes, she told me. Do you want to tell me in your own words?"

"Mum always makes such a drama of everything. I kissed Ana, it's true. But does that make me a certain thing from now until the day I die?"

"So – aren't you?"

"Aren't I what, Dad?"

"Um…"

"Say it."

"Aren't you…gay?"

"I don't know, you tell me. Ana is my friend. She asked me to kiss her and I wanted to kiss her, nothing more than that. I wanted to know what it was like. Does that make me gay, Dad? If so, why don't all those men I kissed make me the opposite?"

"*All* those men?"

"Dad…"

"Sorry."

"I kissed a few men, and I kissed a woman – do I have to know now who I'll want to kiss for the rest of my life?"

"No, nobody knows who they'll want to kiss for the rest of their life."

"But Mum's forcing me into that decision. Mum's waiting for me to announce that I'm gay, and I can't tell her that I am to get her off my back, because the truth is that I really don't know what I am at the moment. Is she going to stick a label on me with each new thing I try? If I smoke a joint I'm going to be a drug addict, if I get drunk I'm going to be an alcoholic, if I go out with more than five blokes I'm going to be a whore. I kissed a friend, Dad, that's what happened, nothing more, I swear."

"You don't have to swear anything to me," he says, and for a while they sit in silence. Pablo's wondering how many things, even if done only once in a lifetime, confer a label on the doer. Is Barletta a "thief" because he stole a

Keith Jarrett CD that summer in Villa Gesell? Is Leonor a "squatter" because she's living in a flat that isn't hers? What label would befit someone who has buried a man (a dead one?) in sordid circumstances and without involving the police? "Accomplice"? What label applies to Marta and Borla, after the events of that night? The same for both? And is he already labelled "adulterer", having slept with Leonor Corell a few hours earlier? Is Laura already a "wronged woman"?

"Haven't you ever kissed a man, Dad?" Francisca asks him, interrupting his reverie.

"No, never," he says, trying to conceal the shock he feels at being asked such a question by his daughter.

"Why not?"

"Because I haven't, because it never came up, because I was always attracted to women, I don't know…"

"Do you think I'm a lesbian, like Mum does?"

"No, no, Francisca, I don't think anything. Or rather, I think the same as you: that you don't know, that almost nobody knows."

"What am I in your eyes?"

"You're my daughter, my little girl."

"Ana says that she knows for sure, that she's never liked boys."

"She probably does know, then."

"Probably."

Cautiously Pablo moves towards her, crouches beside her and hugs her. She lets herself be hugged and starts to cry on his shoulder.

"Will you stay beside me until I go to sleep?" Francisca asks.

"Yes, I'll stay."

The girl slips out of his arms, turns off the computer and gets into bed. Pablo switches off the light, sits beside her and takes her hand. Francisca sobs a little, but gradually the rhythm of her breathing calms and finally she falls asleep. Pablo looks at her, kisses her hand and tucks away a strand of hair that has fallen across her face. Pulling the sheet up to cover her shoulders, he kisses her hand again. And as he sits there on the edge of his daughter's bed, he realizes that he feels neither pity nor concern for her. He gazes at her – he can't stop gazing at her – and wishes he could find a word for what he feels. Respect? Admiration? Yes, he thinks, it's that: he admires his daughter. He, even if he had wanted to, would never have dared to kiss another man.

17

He gets up early. It's Sunday and the likelihood is that Laura and Francisca – unless last night's episode has altered their respective biorhythms – will sleep on until midday. He fetches the newspaper from the doormat outside and goes to have breakfast in the kitchen, taking Jara's notebook too. The book about him. He places it on the table next to the cup into which he's going to pour his coffee when it's ready. He looks at it, still not daring to open it. Instead, he begins with the newspaper; Sunday papers have more and more advertising and that irritates him. He quickly skips over the advertisements for domestic appliances and reads the international news, the politics sections, sports. Most of this he scans; none of the headings draw him into reading the whole piece. His gaze falls on the book again. He looks at his photograph on the book's cover. He looks at the purple stripes on the shirt he's wearing in the photo. He goes to check if the coffee is ready yet. He pours it out, leaves it to cool a little. He drinks it. He opens the cover of the book and on the first page finds the following lines:

Pablo Simó is an architect, married (Laura) and with a daughter (Francisca). He was born in Lanús in 1962 and has no siblings; his parents are dead. He's been in full-time employment since graduation. He is not an associate of the Borla architectural practice despite having worked there for nearly twenty years.

It's chilling enough that Nelson Jara should have known details of his life including the name of his daughter and wife and whether or not his parents are living, but the passage that most reverberates in his head is "He's been in full-time employment since graduation. He is not an associate…" Why did that fact strike Jara as worthy of inclusion in his notebook? Why has Borla never offered to make him an associate? Why has he not demanded it?

And further down:

He takes the underground to work even though this entails a much longer and less direct journey than he would make by bus. Either the traffic bothers him or he likes burying himself alive beneath the city.

The traffic never bothered him. So does he choose the underground in order to bury himself alive? A living man under the city. A living man beneath the earth. If there were even a remote possibility of Jara not being dead when he buried him, then his label shouldn't be "accomplice" but "murderer". He'll never know now which of these he is. How many people have been buried alive in the soil of Buenos Aires? How many deaths that nobody ever found out about? How many deaths denied? Tano Barletta used to claim that when the underground was built the workers who died on the job were buried there and then, in the tunnels that they themselves had dug, through which rails would later pass and, over them, Pablo Simó in a compartment en route to his destination. And he also said that there were corpses buried under the motorway between Buenos

187

Aires and Ezeiza airport. And under what was once the Ital Park funfair. And under the Costanera Sur, in amongst the rubble of demolished houses from San Telmo that was used to fill land reclaimed from the river to create an ecological reserve.

"What can you expect of a city where so many of the dead lie outside the cemetery walls?" Barletta used to complain.

Pablo Simó flicks a few pages on and alights on this paragraph:

It isn't known whether he pursues relationships outside his marriage, which football team he supports or who his friends are.

And a few pages further on there is a chronology of each of their meetings: the first time at the studio ("*Simó is upset by any change in the arrangement of objects on his desk*"; "*He worries about the shoes people wear*"), the afternoon of Jara's fruitless wait at the main entrance ("*Simó spied on me from the corner, he knows that I was there and he knows that he neglected to receive me*") and the coffee on that last occasion at Las Violetas ("*Today Simó was incapable of looking me in the eye*"). Beneath each date and description there is a summary. The one after the first meeting reads:

Pablo Simó is an obsessive perfectionist. At times he believes that he ought to be hard and he attempts this, as if someone had taught him that these are the rules of the game. But it isn't in his nature to be like that. He's more on this side than on the side of the others. A potential friend? An ally?

And then a paragraph that Jara wrote the afternoon he had waited at the main entrance:

There is something disconcerting about Pablo Simó's behaviour.
He seems to be on my side and says he's going to help, but then
he doesn't. Is he a liar? A coward? Is he under pressure from
his boss? If he were only a bit more open I would have offered
him a cut of whatever we manage to get from Borla. Why do I
like Pablo Simó?

The description of their last meeting at Las Violetas is written in telegraphic form – short sentences shorn of detail,
almost as if Jara had been obliged to record it, but had had
neither the enthusiasm nor the time for his task. And the
conclusion is as follows:

Alone again. I was wrong: I can't count on Pablo Simó. So it
will have to be without an ally. Simó is on this side, but he seems
not to know it. The die is cast.

And then the word "*End*", which holds Pablo's gaze. The
end for him and the end for Nelson Jara.

Soon afterwards Pablo calls Leonor, waking her up: it's
still early on this Sunday morning. She says it doesn't matter, that she was about to get up to go for a bicycle ride
with a friend. A friend, Pablo says to himself, and he asks
her if there are any other notebooks in the box, if there is
a notebook for Borla and one for Marta Horvat. Leonor
says she doesn't think there is, but that she is going to check
and will let him know, and she asks if she can call him at
this number. He says yes and prepares to wait for her call.

"No, there aren't any other personal notebooks in that
box. But there are books in the others."

"What others?"

"I've still got two or three other boxes – I threw away the
others. I couldn't hang on to so much paper."

"So what's in the other boxes?"

"They seem to correspond to other buildings. The papers are similar to those ones I showed you, but there are loads of them. They all have a label on the front with an address, a date and an amount in dollars. On your one the sum isn't filled in. There's a space for it but no figure. On all of them there are photographs with cracked walls, diagrams showing the cracks, and newspaper cuttings. And in each of those boxes there is a book with someone's name and a photograph. Would you like me to have a look and tell you the names?"

"No, that's not necessary," says Pablo. He thanks her and hangs up.

Nelson Jara, a one-man crack squad. That could be his label. A professional fraudster. A swindler of architects. One or all of these things. Pablo smiles to himself; he can't help but feel a sneaking sympathy for this man who tricked so many of his colleagues, himself included. It's a shame he's dead, otherwise he'd like to take Jara for a coffee and have him spill all the details. Which studio he got the most money from. Which crack was the hardest to make. He would ask if anyone ever caught him out. How he chose his victims – if that is what they were. How he chose this as a way to make a living. What his retirement plans were. But Jara isn't around and the questions will have to go unanswered. He looks again at the lines that man wrote about him and uses them as the basis to write his own CV, after the word "*End*":

Pablo Simó is a frustrated architect who, despite having very little to lose, panics at the thought of moving beyond the places where he is established: his work, his marriage, his life without music, friends, a football team to cheer for on Sundays, without lovers and without love. He knows very little about himself: that he has a daughter he loves, that he buried a man in the foundations of a building, that he would like to construct an eleven-storey, north-facing tower block, that he fears he will never make that eleven-storey tower and that, until today, he was stuck on the side to which he didn't belong.

He looks at what he has written and sees that almost unintentionally he has mimicked Nelson Jara's handwriting. With a bit of practice he could replicate it exactly, he thinks. At that moment Laura comes into the kitchen. Her eyes are swollen from hours of crying and her expression suggests she plans to cry again, once her tear ducts have recuperated.

"Could you sleep?" she asks.

"Not much, but a bit."

"Men are lucky, almost nothing keeps them awake."

"Don't you believe it. I've had many sleepless nights."

"When?"

"Lots of times, during all these years we've been together."

"I never realized."

"You were asleep!"

"Well, it would have been for some minor thing; nothing as serious as this has ever happened to us before."

"Speak for yourself."

"What do you mean? Are you going to tell me that something as serious as this has happened to you and I never found out about it?"

"A few years ago I buried a man under the cement of a building that we had under construction. I still don't know today whether that man was alive or dead. On your scale of serious events, which would rank higher, Laura: Francisca's sexuality or me burying a man alive?"

18

On Monday before entering the studio Pablo goes for his usual coffee, a prerequisite for starting the day. Open in front of him is the notebook Nelson Jara dedicated to him. It doesn't matter which page is in front of his eyes because this time Pablo Simó isn't focusing on the content, on what the words say, but on the writing itself, the strokes that Nelson Jara effected with a steady hand and painstaking calligraphy. He notices that the "o" and the "a" shaped by this man are almost identical except in their final curlicue, that they have the same degree of slant towards the right, the same size of ellipsis, and that the "t" extends higher than Simó's own "t" – when he writes "Marta", for example – and the "p" also extends lower than his own "p". Pablo tries copying Jara's writing on a paper napkin. He writes, "What would happen if…?" And again, "What would happen if…?" And then, "happen". And "happen", again. And he tries out the question mark. "What would happen if one afternoon…?" "…one afternoon." "if one afternoon…" "…afternoon…".

He looks at the clock: it's time to go to work. He pays for the coffee, picks up Jara's notebook and leaves, but even as he's arriving at the door to the studio, he realizes that he has left on the table the napkin on which he was practising letters and goes back to get it. That's when Leonor, approaching on a bicycle, has to swerve to avoid crashing into him.

"Hello!" she says.

"Hello!" he says. "Are you going for a ride?"

"No, I'm going to work."

"By bike…"

"Yes, I'm sick of the bus. The traffic in this city gets worse and worse and I get later and later to work. Don't you find the same thing?"

"I go by underground."

"Of course – I read that in your notes."

Pablo blushes as it dawns on him that Leonor must have read everything that Jara wrote about him in the exercise book. He hesitates between clearing up a few details, refuting others, denying the whole thing, or saying nothing and accepting the portrait as essentially accurate. He decides to ask her:

"The other day, at your house" – and it moves him to say "your house" – "you said that you wanted to ask me something about what Jara says about me in the notebook."

"Oh yes, true. Shall I ask you now?"

"Go on then."

"Has there really never been another woman in your life since you got married?"

"It depends what's meant by the phrase 'another woman in your life'."

"That you've been with another woman; that you've been in love."

"No. Up until the time Jara wrote that there hadn't been, no."

"And afterwards there was?"

"That's not part of our pact. I agreed to answer questions to do with the notebook. A deal's a deal."

"You're right."

"Coward," says Barletta, but Pablo pretends not to see or hear him.

For a moment there is silence between them; both are uncomfortable, not knowing what else to say. When they do opt to speak it's at the same time and what one says is lost in the other's murmur.

"Do you want to see how the project came out?" she says while he is saying, "So you've bought a bicycle?"

Leonor laughs at the mix-up, making Pablo laugh in turn.

"Go ahead," the girl says.

"No – you first," says Pablo.

"I was asking if you would like to see the end result of my photographic project. I've got it in the rucksack," she says, pointing to the one on her back that Pablo knows so well.

"Is it finished already?"

"Yes, I have to hand it in today."

"Oh, I thought that perhaps…another day…"

Without waiting for him to finish the sentence – something Pablo wouldn't have done anyway – the girl takes the rucksack off her back, opens it, pulls out a folder and passes it to him. On the folder there's a title, "Five Faces of a City", and her name, Leonor Corell. Pablo opens the folder and looks through it. He's not an expert in photography but he likes what he sees and would even say that these are good photographs. Leonor has given each of them a caption: 1) Men who labour in vain; 2) Head with lilies; 3) Peacocks, some displaying their tails (the only caption on the page where she had stuck the three Colombo façades); 4) Railing in Barrio Norte; 5) Liberty with dry-cleaners.

Pablo wonders how he would have titled them. Looking through the pictures again, mentally he gives them captions: 1) The first time I really looked at Leonor; 2) She and I sit together on a car boot; 3) Stubborn Blood – a seventeen-year age gap; 4) Leonor among Spanish ironwork; 5) Leonor invites me to her house.

"What do you think?" she asks.

"It's turned out really well," he answers, and hands her back the folder.

"Did you see this?" Leonor asks him, and holds the folder open on the last page so that he can read, "With special thanks to the architect Pablo Simó."

Pablo stares at his name written in Leonor's hand.

If he could, he would caress his name handwritten by Leonor; he would trace the blue-ink letters with his index finger, but he knows he can't do this in front of her, so he simply thanks her and hands back the folder for her to put it away. As she bends down to put the folder in her rucksack her hair falls over her face, and Pablo realizes that she isn't wearing her hair tied up today and that he likes it that way. And that he also likes her T-shirt, which is similar to the ones she always wears, her worn jeans and her high-top canvas trainers, which she was also wearing the first time they met.

"And what were you saying?"

"When?"

"Just now, when we both started talking at the same time."

"I don't remember."

"Something about a bicycle, I think."

"Oh yes, I was asking if you'd bought this bicycle."

"No, it's Damian's. We went out for a ride yesterday and he left it at mine."

"Who's Damian?"

"My boyfriend."

"Bitch," says Barletta, and Pablo wonders why his friend has to choose this moment to appear.

"My ex-boyfriend, really. The one from Mar del Plata."

"Oh, so you still see each other," he says.

"Yes, we're cool, totally."

"And he left his bike with you. So he's coming back."

"Yes, he comes round all the time. Or I go there."

"They're like that, brother," says Barletta, putting an arm around his shoulder. "Girls are like that these days – free. You want them to be yours alone but you have to be content with just a bit of them because the alternative is nothing. They're free, beautiful – and bitches."

Pablo changes position, hoping to make Barletta disappear. He doesn't feel like having an argument with him about what Leonor Corell is or isn't like.

"Can I ask you something?" he says to the girl.

"Yes."

"I need you to look among Jara's papers for something for me."

"What sort of thing?"

"A sheet of paper where you can see his handwriting really well, like a report about the building or the crack, talking about the work but not about me."

"I'll have a look and let you know. I'm sure there's something like that."

"I need it quite urgently."

"I'll look tonight."

They both fall silent again for a moment, then Leonor straightens her bicycle, aligns the pedals so they're ready to go and says goodbye.

"OK, I'd better go or I'll end up being late today, as well. I'll send you that thing as soon as I find it," she says, getting onto the bike and riding away.

"Thanks, and good luck at work," Pablo shouts as she cycles away and he is left to admire the way her hair fans over her back.

"It wasn't after all, then", says Barletta.

"It wasn't what?" he replies.

"Love."

Pablo hesitates, watching Leonor until she is out of sight.

"No," he says finally, when he can't see her any more. "If she was love, she never knew it."

"Yet again it wasn't to be."

"Yet again."

"And now where are you going to look for it?"

"For what?"

"For love."

"I'm not going to look for it any more. If it's somewhere out there, I suppose it will send a sign."

"A sign? What kind of sign?"

"A clear and distinct one."

19

Pablo spends all day at the studio, as though nothing has happened. There's less work around these days: although there are various jobs with feasibility reports started, the financial insecurity in some country's stock market, or in all countries that have a stock market – he can never quite understand how their effects reach Calle Giribone – have caused investment in property development to be suspended over the next few months.

"We're on standby, Pablo, waiting for things to settle down," says Borla when he comes by the office that afternoon, and he asks Pablo, "What do you think of what's happening in the markets?"

But if there is one thing that Pablo is not even the slightest bit interested in at this moment in his life, it is what's happening "in the markets". What exactly are the markets? Who are the markets? Where are they? Can you touch them, like he touched Leonor Corell? Or like he touched the crack in Jara's apartment? Can they be thrown into a footing and have cement poured over them? Well then, don't come and talk to him about the markets.

"Anything else to report?" Borla asks before going into his office.

"Not for the moment, everything's fine," Pablo answers.

Marta Horvat doesn't even come to the studio. It's been a while since she and Pablo crossed paths. He knows that she's starting on a new job this week – the last to be approved by Borla, right before the crisis, if that is what it is – and the smell of churned-up earth, the lorries unloading supplies, the chit-chat of the workers who answer to her, all of this exerts such a strong attraction on Marta that she often doesn't set foot on solid ground for weeks.

In free moments, Pablo Simó tries again to master Jara's handwriting style. "What would happen if…" "What would happen…" "…if one afternoon…" "because that night…" "That night…" "…an error…" "…there was an error…" "What would happen if…"

Towards the end of the day, Pablo takes out his folder of sketches and once more draws the eleven-storey north-facing tower. He draws it the same as always: the same façade, the same windows, the same layout, the same entrance. But this time, when the sketch is finished, he counts the floors and pauses at the fifth. He chooses one of the windows at random and draws in a crack, almost invisible to the human eye on this scale, but real. It's really there and nobody can deny it because he drew it, from top to bottom, from left to right, approximating as closely as he could the crack he remembers crossing the wall of the apartment where Jara once lived and where Leonor lives now.

That evening when he leaves the studio, rather than descending into the underground he walks a few blocks and goes into two or three property agencies to ask about flats available to rent.

"Something small, two rooms, or three at the most. Small and cheap. And furnished, if possible."

They show him pictures of properties matching the requirements he describes. Pablo barely glances at these, considering them only briefly in order to feign an interest in the look of the places worth renting; then he closes his eyes and presses them with his fingers, as if he had a headache or was tired, and meanwhile he tries to remember the block in which each of these flats is. Some of them he can place, others not; it's easier when the apartments are in areas he knows from scoping out potential sites for Borla. If memory serves, the one they offer him half a block away from Avenida Federico Lacroze could be next to some land they tried to buy from a school that had started to teeter after the 2001 crisis and closed for good three years later, but another architectural practice beat them to it. And the one in Calle Tronador, he's practically sure, is next to an early twentieth-century mansion that was demolished a few months ago and where there's already a security fence and site board. He jots down the addresses of the ones that interest him; he doesn't leave his own details but promises to call to arrange an interview and to view the apartments personally. Back on the street after visiting the last agency, he decides to use what's left of the daylight to have a look at the apartments he has noted down. The one on the corner of Federico Lacroze turns out not to be next to the school plot they wanted to buy and couldn't secure – there's a house and another building between them – but the one on Tronador is indeed next to that demolished mansion where Garrido and Associates Architects are in the process of building some duplexes – very upmarket ones, if the hoarding is to be believed. Luckily, he doesn't know Garrido. He finds a phone booth and makes an appointment to see the apartment the next day. Then he looks for the nearest underground station and plunges in, on his way back home.

This time he goes straight home, without pausing to have his last coffee of the day. Entering the flat, he's relieved to find nobody in the living room, so he can go straight to the bathroom, putting off greetings and explanations, to wash his face, wash it again, then dry it with a white towel, not rubbing his skin but giving it gentle, brief pats, and then stay there for a few minutes looking at himself in the mirror.

Next he goes looking for Laura. He finds her in the room that has, until now, been the marital suite, shared for twenty years. He tells her that he's leaving, that he's decided they should separate. She doesn't believe him: first she laughs, then she gets angry and shouts at him, orders him to sleep in the living room that night – not because she sees that they are indeed separating, but because she treats Pablo like a little boy and this is a punishment to stop him being silly – and finally she tells him to get out and shuts herself in the room with a slam. Laura seems convinced that her husband's announcement is a hangover from the argument they had the other day after she fought with Francisca, and evidently wants to tell him so before going to bed. She appears in the kitchen, in her nightgown, just as he is warming up something to eat.

"We're on edge because of what this child is putting us through. The worst thing would be for that to end up affecting our relationship too."

And without waiting for his response or observations she goes back to her room, as though gifting him this maxim as something to reflect on. Pablo is left with the words of his wife playing in his head. But does Laura believe that their relationship has not yet been affected? Does she believe that this life they've led for the last twenty years can still be called that of a couple? Is it enough to say that whatever can be jointly administered without too much inconvenience – bills, a home, breakfasts and dinners, the odd conversation, a bed where not much happens, the television, the education of their daughter, a bank account and health insurance – constitutes a couple? Their relationship mustn't be affected, Laura says, and Pablo knows that it won't be because the relationship to which she refers no longer exists. He's known this for a while, although he hasn't dared to admit it even to himself because there are certain "truths" – that Father Christmas exists, that the Tooth Fairy cares as much about the number of teeth we lose as she likes paying for them, that teachers love all their children equally, that love can last a lifetime – that we find hard to stop believing in even when the evidence, such as Mummy hiding the presents under the tree, is really incontrovertible.

While Laura sleeps, that same night, Pablo goes to their room and, making as little noise as possible, starts to pack a suitcase with a few essentials. The following morning, a little before his daughter gets up to go to school, he goes to her room to talk to her. He explains that he is looking for a place to live because her mother and he have decided to separate, trying to follow as closely as possible what he imagines to be the guidelines of modern psychology in relation to childcare. But Francisca isn't easily convinced.

"Is it because of what happened the other day?" she asks. "Because of what happened with Ana?"

He reassures her that their decision has nothing to do with her, that it's a decision her mother and he should have made a long time ago. And Pablo is firm, emphatic: he wants to leave no room for doubts that might lead his daughter to take on board a guilt that isn't hers. He thinks he's said enough to leave the matter closed, but Francisca asks him:

"Why?"

"Because being married is something that has stopped making us happy."

"No, I'm not asking why you're getting separated. I'm asking why that happens, why one day you don't love someone any more, why you stop being happy with them. Will that happen to me, too?"

Pablo wants to say no, that it won't happen to her, that she's going to fall in love and the feeling will last forever. Francisca living the whole life stretching ahead of her with the same person. He thinks of that and it scares him, and he asks himself if that really would be a mark of determination – a whole life spent with the same person – or simply of a kind of resignation. Because life is long, and getting longer, and love is so difficult to recognize in the midst of all the fireworks and glowing embers.

"I don't know, darling. But you're going to be happy. I'm sure that, whoever you end up with, you'll know how to be happy."

Francisca doesn't ask him anything else. He's about to go, but before he does he corrects himself on a previous point. He says that in a way she did have something to do with the decision they made – at least on his side – because she showed him that it is possible to do what you want without all the planets falling out of the sky.

"And if they do, we'll have to go and ask Professor Hawking what happened, because it certainly won't be anything to do with us."

Francisca laughs:

"Do you know anything about Stephen Hawking?"

"Nothing," he admits, and then both of them laugh, but immediately afterwards she looks serious.

"What's wrong?" he asks her.

"Promise me that as soon as you have somewhere to live, you'll take me with you."

Pablo doesn't answer; he can't, he has a lump in his throat. But he nods, several times, and when he's certain of being able to speak without his voice catching, he says:

"I promise you."

And he isn't lying.

He goes over to her, kisses her forehead and says:

"I'd better go and let you get dressed. I don't want to make you late for school."

Pablo leaves her room and waits in the kitchen. Usually by this time in the morning he would be underground on his way to work, but today he wants to wait for Laura, who took more tablets than usual last night, to wake up.

"So it's true?" she says, soon afterwards, looking at the suitcase, her eyes filling with tears.

"Yes."

"Can I ask why?"

"Because I can't think of a reason for us to keep living together."

"Being married isn't enough?"

"No."

"I don't know what makes you think you're so special, Pablo. Tell me, how many couples do you know who have a reason to keep living together beyond the fact of being married? That's a stupid, romantic concept of marriage."

"I've always been stupid. Perhaps I'm starting now to be romantic."

"At your age it's not going to be a good look."

Pablo prefers to keep his silence. He can't think of anything else to say; he would only be going back and forth over the ground Laura and he covered last night. Anyway, it may be that on this point she is right, that romanticism looks ridiculous in a man of his age. Is Laura exactly the person he sees today? Is Laura the person he has known these last eleven thousand and seventy days together? Or might there be another Laura that Pablo hasn't yet been able to discover? Has she other aspects of her character to bring out, could she be a different kind of woman if she were with another man, or on her own? Pablo suspects that daily routine and the passing years have made a trap for her, that Laura is more than the woman he sees, but that the trap is fatal and inescapable.

"Is there someone else? Have you got another woman, Pablo?" she asks, and for the first time her voice breaks.

"No, Laura, I haven't got another woman. I've got nothing – just this suitcase and that dead man I told you about, the one I buried under the cement."

"Oh yes, the famous corpse. You thought you could trick me, right? You underestimated me. That dead man doesn't exist. You told me that because you thought a story like that would make me want to leave you. But now you see it didn't work, I haven't left you. I'm made of sterner stuff. Through thick and thin. Corpse or no corpse. If you want a separation, you're going to have to be the one to leave."

"That's what I'm doing," says Pablo and, picking up his suitcase, he walks out of the door.

Francisca catches up with him on the landing. She hands him a CD.

"It's Leonard Cohen. I haven't made a recording for you yet, but take mine, and I'll get another one later."

"Thanks."

"Remember your promise."

"I remember, and I'll keep it. I'll call you as soon as I have a place to sleep."

She comes closer and hugs him.

"I love you," Francisca says, close to his ear.

"I love you," he says to her.

Francisca turns to go back into the apartment, trying not to let him see that this time she's the one about to cry. Are they also similar in this respect, his daughter and he? In hiding their tears? Pablo gets into the lift, presses the ground-floor button, and holding on tight to his suitcase feels the beginning of its descent in the pit of his stomach.

Watching the floors pass, he wonders when the last time was that somebody said "I love you" to him, or that he said it to anyone. He can find no answer. Even as he arrives at the ground floor, he can't think when the last time was.

20

He arrives at the office a little later than usual, carrying his suitcase. He puts it in the storeroom, next to some rolls of carpet left over from the redecorating Borla did in his apartment and which his wife wanted to get out of the way, together with some furniture they used in the last showroom. On his way back to his desk he inadvertently kicks an envelope that has been slid under the door. The envelope reads: From Leonor, for Pablo Simó. He wonders whether the girl came by recently, while he was in the storeroom, and preferred not to stay and say hello, or whether the envelope was already there on the floor when he arrived a few minutes ago and he simply didn't see it. He opens it. Inside is the paper he had asked Leonor for – a detailed description of the crack's progress day by day – and, to his surprise, several photos from that Saturday they spent together: him trying to take the camera away from her in front of the Liberty building, him sticking his tongue out beside the door to the dry-cleaners, and three other photographs that the girl must have taken without Pablo realizing: one crossing Avenida Rivadavia, another of him hailing the taxi and a third next to the graffiti extolling Stubborn Blood. A little pink slip of paper, clipped onto one of the photos, reads, "Thanks for everything, Leonor."

Pablo's attention is held by this note. Although it doesn't say so, the text reads like a farewell. He puts the document written by Jara into an envelope he labels "Nelson Jara's papers", and puts that away in the bottom drawer of his desk – somewhere it can easily be found when he no longer works there – and then he adds the photos with the little pink note to the folder of sketches of the building he plans to make one day.

Next, he looks for a blank sheet of paper and writes:

What would happen if one afternoon I paid you a visit? What if one of these days you discover that I am still alive? That there was a fundamental fact you didn't know and still don't know, and that is that when you threw me into the footing I hadn't died yet and that fate, distraction or human error allowed me to climb out before you tipped your damned cement on top of me? Well, we shall soon see, because any day now I'm coming to see you, to bring you personally my very cordial and sincere greetings, greetings I've been keeping to myself for three years.

Nelson Jara

Pablo opens the drawer to his desk, looks inside the envelope that Leonor sent him with Jara's handwriting and checks that the "y" hasn't come out as badly as he thought. Then he looks for another envelope and in the same handwriting he writes Architectural Director Borla, Associate Architect Marta Horvat, Non-Associate Architect Pablo Simó. He places the note that he has just written inside the envelope, licks the glue on the flap and closes the envelope. Then he puts it in his pocket: this afternoon he'll have time to go to the post office and send it.

When Borla arrives, Simó requests a meeting; the architect seems surprised by this formality, but of course he agrees.

"Come to my office in five minutes. Oh, and bring a couple of coffees with you."

Ten minutes later, Pablo goes to Borla's office carrying a coffee.

"You're not having one?" his boss asks, putting sugar into his cup and stirring it.

And he says no, that he only drinks espressos, short and very strong. Borla's utter lack of interest in Pablo's taste in coffee is evident, but he articulates it even so:

"What did you want to talk to me about, Pablo? I'm guessing this isn't about coffee, right?"

"No, no, Mario. I wanted to let you know that I'm going to be leaving the practice."

"What?"

"Simply that, that I won't be working with you any more."

"Why not?"

"I'm making some changes in my life; I want to do some of the things I haven't had a chance to do up until now."

"Such as? Walking across the Andes or climbing the Lanín volcano?" Pablo doesn't answer and Borla continues, "I have a friend who threw in everything at the age of forty to go and climb Lanín – you know? – and at forty-one he was back at the same lawyers' firm as before, but on a slightly lower salary."

"No, I'm not going to climb Lanín. I'm going to build a tower block."

"Seriously?"

"Yes, I've had one in mind for a long time."

"Well why don't you bring me the project? If it's worthwhile we'll do it."

"I don't think you would find it worthwhile."

"Well if you're not convinced by your own project…"

"I certainly am convinced by it, but it's not the sort of project that would be of interest to everyone."

"Are you thinking of putting the money up yourself?"

"Why did you never make me an associate?"

"On a project?"

"No, in this practice."

"Because…I don't know, because it wasn't necessary, because you never asked for it. Do you want to be an associate? If that's the issue…I don't know, perhaps with a symbolic percentage."

"No, not any more. Now I want to leave."

"And when will you go?"

"I don't know…in a few days."

"You can't leave me stranded from one day to the next."

"The thing is, I need to get straight to work."

"And you already have another job?"

"Something of my own. With the money I make from that I can start saving for the tower block I want to put up."

"Ah, well you must be onto something good. Is it something within our profession or an undertaking in some other kind of business?"

"Within this profession, or rather, related to this profession."

"Related to the profession – yes, that's a good sideline. Architecture itself, as they taught it to us in the faculty, isn't a viable business any more, but there are lots of possibilities 'related' to architecture these days. Let me know the details sometime – I might like to get involved myself."

"OK. When I've got it up and running I'll let you know."

"Give me a few days to find a replacement. Can I count on you for that?"

"Yes, so long as it's only for a few days."

Their conversation is over, but Pablo doesn't leave. He feels that something is missing, that, after so many years as colleagues, their farewell ought to end with a hug, with a meaningful handshake or with a punch-up. Should he take the initiative, walk the few paces between them and embrace Borla – or hit him? It seems to make his boss uncomfortable that Pablo is still standing there without saying anything.

"Right, well…that's settled, then," he says.

"Yes, absolutely," Pablo says finally, and he leaves Borla's office.

At lunchtime he goes to the property agency and signs a rental contract on the apartment in Calle Tronador, but, in spite of his protests, they say it's not possible for him to move in until the following day. He hadn't bargained on having to find somewhere else to spend that night. Walking back to the studio from the agency, he stops at a post office to post the envelope in his pocket – with a second-class stamp so that it arrives after he has left the studio – and he feels that everything is finally moving in the right direction.

A little later, on the corner of Céspedes and Alvarez Thomas, a man who's crossing the street and pushing a pram waves to him. Pablo has the strange sensation of knowing the man without having the slightest idea who he is. The man is very overweight and his remaining hair encircles a recent but undeniable bald patch. This hair – long, wispy and grey – is worn in a ponytail. He's sporting office clothes – a white shirt, tie and grey trousers without a jacket – all of it rumpled and bad quality. The man looks too old to have such a small baby, but too young to be a grandfather. There are sweat marks on his shirt, around his chest. And this man is now making for him with determination.

"Pablo Simó, am I right, brother?" he says, and before Pablo can answer, the man's embracing him.

Hearing the word "brother" is enough to tip Pablo off that the man before him is Tano Barletta.

"You haven't changed," his friend says.

"Neither have you," Pablo lies, for the Barletta who pops into his mind every so often had been frozen at twenty-four or twenty-five years old. "The baby's yours?"

"Yes, our little accident. I've got two more – they're over there with my wife," he says, and points towards a bar.

"So you finally got married…"

"Ah yes, well what choice is there? Eventually you get tired of being alone."

"And where are you working?" Pablo asks him.

"In a factory that makes office furniture. It's good work, good quality furniture, big clients, you know – important."

"You design furniture?"

"No, I'm more on the marketing side of things, you know?"

"I think so."

"I sell, basically. I visit the clients, assess their needs and sell to them."

"And are you happy?"

"Yes, yes…well, happy in that I've got work, the family is well – what more can you ask for?"

"No, you can't really ask for more than that, can you?"

They're both silent for a moment, looking at each other. Chalk and cheese, thinks Pablo, even now, twenty years on, and he wonders what Tano Barletta's impression of them both is, at this moment.

"Here comes my wife. Wait and I'll introduce you."

Barletta explains who Pablo is to his wife and she shakes hands with him, and makes her children do likewise. From

212

her reaction, Pablo realizes that Tano has probably never spoken to her about him, or if he has she doesn't remember it. The two older children start hitting each other and Barletta delivers a sharp but gentle smack to the head nearest to him.

"Hey, don't make me look bad in front of my friend," he says.

They exchange a few more awkward pleasantries so as not to cut the meeting short there.

"I'll give you my number," Barletta says, and hands him a card with the logo of the office supplies company for which he works. "Call me and we'll get together for a meal, OK? We can relive the old days. We had some great times together, didn't we?"

"Yes, we had a good time," Pablo says.

Barletta, his wife and children are already crossing Avenida Álvarez Thomas when Tano turns round and shouts:

"Say hello to Laura and your daughter."

"Thanks," he calls back.

In the afternoon, Pablo goes to say goodbye to Marta Horvat. Entering the site, he stops just inside the security fence and observes from a distance, perhaps for the last time, her interaction with the workers. She is their queen, he thinks, the queen of those men who run back and forth with bricks, cables, trowels, picks and shovels. But even though the passing years have been much kinder to her than to other women – and she is still one of the most beautiful he has ever known – Marta Horvat no longer bewitches Pablo Simó in the way she once did. Why, he wonders, why can he look at her now without needing to imagine her naked, why does he no longer feel jealous of the men moving around close to her, why does his body not signal an alert when in

213

proximity to Marta Horvat's body, as it has done so many times before? Is the desire awakened by a woman also a firework that goes out, the same as love?

Pablo walks towards her and, for the first time, isn't scared that she's about to humiliate him.

"What are you doing here?" Marta asks.

"I came to say goodbye. I'm leaving the practice," says Pablo and he could swear – could it really be? – that the news comes as an unwelcome surprise to her.

"No, no, I can't believe it…you're not serious."

"Yes, Marta, I really am."

"But why? Why are you going?"

"I'm going to build that tower block you've seen me draw thousands of times in the studio. And please don't tell me again that the plot ratio isn't in my favour," he says, and Marta, to his surprise, smiles.

"I swear I never told you the plot ratio wasn't in your favour."

"I swear you did."

"God, I'm terrible."

"Yes, you're terrible."

Pablo has the impression that Marta Horvat's eyes are filling with tears. In fact she lowers the sunglasses that had been perched on her head even though the sun, at that time of day, can't be bothering her any more.

"How old are you, Pablo?" she asks, and the question surprises him.

"Forty-five."

"Three years younger than me," says Marta, who thinks for a moment then continues. "Do you think there is still time to turn the wheel and set a different course?"

"I've hit an iceberg. I've got no option but to change course."

214

"You were lucky – sometimes it's necessary to hit an iceberg," she tells him, and he wonders if the letter he wrote in Jara's handwriting could end up being the iceberg that Marta Horvat needs.

And then, surpassing any expectation that Simó could have had even at the best times, Marta comes close, hugs him and stays for a moment pressed against him; then she gives him a quick kiss on the cheek and, as though embarrassed by such a display of affection, she quickly says goodbye:

"Well, I'll let you get on, I have a lot to do. Good luck, Pablo. If you need anything, you know where I am."

She's already walking away by the time she finishes speaking and so she doesn't hear Pablo when he says:

"I know where you are, yes."

Pablo returns to the studio after everyone else has left – not just from his office but from almost all the others in the block. Before going up to his floor he buys some slices of pizza and a small bottle of beer. He moves aside the few things left on his desk and uses it as a dinner table. He remembers Nelson Jara's last supper, in that same place, but when the building was still only a promise based on an open pit in the ground. He remembers the leftovers of pizza that he himself cleared away. And Jara's shoes, and the heft of his body, and that hammer – but today he notes that the memories do not weigh as heavily on him as they did, as though, finally, he has made his peace with them. Then he calls Francisca and tells her that that night he will sleep in a hotel, but that he will have a flat the next day and that he will give her the details as soon as possible so that she can find him. She asks if he would like to speak to Laura and he says no, that he would prefer not to speak to her again that day, but that tomorrow he will call her too. After hanging up, he casts a glance around the place, looking at the corners that he will soon not see again. He imagines the moment that Borla receives the envelope sent by Nelson Jara, and that's exactly how he thinks it, "the envelope sent by Nelson Jara", as if the man really existed, as if the man really were about to call on those people who believe him dead and buried. He knows that it will be better for Borla and Marta to read the letter when he is no longer there. It avoids him having to lie to them, pretending that he too is worried by the letter, that he is also alarmed by the thought that Jara is alive. It will save him having to say, "But are you sure that's Jara's handwriting?" and having to open the bottom drawer of his desk, taking out the written sheet for them to compare the handwriting and confirm their worst fears. He goes to the storeroom to get some clothes from his suitcase so as to make a makeshift bed between his desk and Marta Horvat's. He lies down, folding his arms behind his head, and realizes that it is the first time in twenty years that he has looked at the ceiling of his workplace. He studies every corner, every light fitting, every imperfection in the plaster or paintwork.

Finally he closes his eyes and tries to sleep. He knows that tonight he might dream of Marta Horvat, or of Leonor Corell or of Laura or Francisca. If he had a choice, though, he would prefer not to dream, but simply to close his eyes and sleep, without the intervention of any of these women who in different ways and to different degrees have so often infiltrated his dreams. Because tonight he is truly tired, really tired. Tonight he wants nothing of them: not love, or affection, or desire, or "I love you"s, or joined bodies, seeking one another.

Tonight Pablo Simó wants only to close his eyes and be allowed to sleep.

21

Early the following morning, Pablo Simó goes to the property agency to pick up the keys for the apartment he's rented, carrying his suitcase and the file with the sketches of the north-facing eleven-storey tower. And not long afterwards he is opening the door to the place where he plans to spend the next few months. He puts his suitcase in the bedroom, then he returns to the living room, opens the window and breathes deeply, letting the sun bathe his face. Making a quick survey of the four cardinal points, he concludes that by the time Garrido and Associates have put up the duplex flats promised on their hoarding, the sun will no longer come through this window as it does today.

There isn't much action on the neighbouring plot, but there's quite a stockpile of materials, and that reassures him; nobody invests in bricks without pressing ahead with the job in hand.

He returns to his room, opens the suitcase and puts on more comfortable clothes: shorts, a T-shirt and trainers. From an inside pocket he takes out his toolbox, then he returns to the living room. He takes from his folder the most recent sketch, the one incorporating Jara's crack. He leans it against the side wall, as though it were a picture that he has not yet had a chance to hang but will, as soon as he has properly moved in. He walks towards the other wall, the party wall, the one bordering the plot where Garrido and Associates will soon be excavating a pit and then cementing the foundations of the duplex building they plan to build. He opens the toolbox, takes out a hammer and chisel, runs his hand over the wall, detecting two or three imperfections in the paintwork, and then, as though this were familiar work, he starts to carve a crack. Patiently he chips at the beginning of this fissure, which he knows is going to grow little by little, by dint of the strokes he makes. Day by day he will take photographs as the crack advances, he will note down its progress in inches, he will carry notebooks in which he records the meetings with enemies and with potential allies. He will measure the width and depth of the crack and he will wait.

He strikes and chips at the wall, strikes and chips, strikes and chips once more.

The dust makes him cough, but he doesn't stop, he will stop only when he has chipped away the amount by which the crack is going to grow that day, according to his own plan.

Then he turns his head over his shoulder and looks for him. He knows that he must be there, and indeed there he is, standing behind him, observing his work.

Pablo Simó looks at him, waiting for an opinion, and Nelson Jara, without saying a word, with a clear movement of his head and a barely insinuated smile, nods.

ALL YOURS

Claudia Piñeiro

Infidelity and obsession lead to murder…

Inés is convinced that every wife is bound to be betrayed one day, so she is not surprised to find a note in her husband Ernesto's briefcase with a heart smeared in lipstick crossed by the words "All Yours". Following him to a park in Buenos Aires on a rainy winter evening, she witnesses a violent quarrel between her husband and another woman. The woman collapses; Ernesto sinks her body in a nearby lake.

When Ernesto becomes a suspect in the case Inés provides him with an alibi. After all, hatred can bring people together as urgently as love. But Ernesto cannot bring his sexual adventures to an end, so Inés concocts a plan for revenge from which there is no return.

"If you read only one crime book in translation this year, make *All Yours* the one, a book that grabs you from the start and whips along at pace. Piñeiro is a best-selling Argentinean author, and unlike many South American books this one doesn't loiter. It screams out to become a film – *The Postman Only Brings Double Indemnity* perhaps". *CrimeTime*

£8.99/$14.95
Crime Paperback Original
ISBN 978 1904738 800
eBook ISBN 978 1904738 817

www.bitterlemonpress.com

THURSDAY NIGHT WIDOWS

Claudia Piñeiro

"A nimble novel, a ruthless dissection of a fast-decaying society"—José Saramago, winner of the Nobel prize for literature

Three bodies lie at the bottom of a swimming pool in a gated country estate near Buenos Aires. Under the gaze of fifteen security guards, the pampered residents of Cascade Heights lead a charmed life of parties and tennis tournaments, ignoring the poverty outside the perimeter wall. Claudia Piñeiro's novel eerily foreshadowed a criminal case that generated a scandal in the Argentine media. But this is more than a tale about crime, it is a psychological portrait of a middle class living beyond its means and struggling to conceal deadly secrets. Set during the post-9/11 economic meltdown in Argentina, this story will resonate among credit-crunched readers of today.

Winner of the Clarín Prize for fiction and now a film by Argentine New Wave director Marcelo Piñeyro.

"A gripping story. The dystopia portrayed is an indictment not solely of an assassin but of Argentina's class structure and the wilful blindness of its petty bourgeoisie." *Times Literary Supplement*

"A fine morality tale which explores the dark places societies enter when they place material comfort before social justice, and security before morality." *Publishers Weekly*

£7.99/$14.95
Crime Paperback Original
ISBN 978 1904738 411
eBook ISBN 978 1904738 589

www.bitterlemonpress.com